The Calendar Man

A Scandinavian Dark Advent novel set in Greenland

~ Petra *Piitalaat* Jensen Book 1 ~

by Christoffer Petersen

CHRISTOFFER PETERSEN

Published by Aarluuk Press

ISBN: 978-87-93680-15-9

Original Cover Photo Annie Spratt
@anniespratt (Unsplash)

www.christoffer-petersen.com

Conceal me what I am, and be my aid
For such disguise as haply shall become
The form of my intent.

— *Twelfth Night, Act I, Sc. II*

William Shakespeare (1564-1616)

Introduction

~ This is not a book ~

The Calendar Man is, however, a complete story, and you can read it like a book, from start to finish, one chapter after another. Or, if you're feeling festive, you can read it in the way it is intended, as a Scandinavian *Julekalender* – a story told over twenty-four days, from December 1st to Christmas Eve on December 24th, the night Greenlanders and Scandinavians celebrate Christmas.

Scandinavian *Julekalendere* (plural) have been a part of the Scandinavian Christmas tradition and culture for decades, and the first *Julekalender* aired on Danish television in 1962. Greenland also has a tradition for *Julekalender*, and I saw one of the first Greenlandic-produced Christmas Calendars called *Ammartagaq* in 2010.

The classic format of the Scandinavian Christmas Calendar tells a story over twenty-four television episodes. The action occurs over the course of each day, and as the month progresses it looks increasingly unlikely that there will be a Christmas this year. This is a common theme in many Christmas stories and films with many variations.

The Calendar Man is my version of a *Julekalender* set in Greenland in the year 2042. It is not science fiction, and there is very little technology or technobabble to distract from the story. However, some current issues, such as Greenlandic independence, the Chinese interest in Greenland's minerals, and the threat of rising sea levels, do play a part, and it was fun to imagine a future Greenland including characters from my existing series of books.

True to the nature of a Christmas Calendar, *The Calendar Man* is episodic, with new events and discoveries that drive the investigation towards its dramatic climax. But unlike Christmas Calendars in Denmark and Greenland, the elves have been replaced, and it is up to the police, and Police Commissioner Petra Jensen, to save Christmas.

The Calendar Man is a Dark Advent story with elements of the Greenlandic Christmas tradition woven into the story.

Whether or not you are familiar with my Greenland crime novels and stories, *The Calendar Man* can be read independently of the other books. Some reference, however, is made to earlier stories, without spoilers, for the sake of continuity.

Remember, it's not a book. Try to limit yourself to one chapter a day.

Merry Christmas!

Chris
December 2018
Denmark

CHRISTOFFER PETERSEN

The Calendar Man

A Scandinavian Dark Advent novel set in Greenland

~ Petra *Piitalaat* Jensen Book 1 ~

Ataasinngorneq

Monday, 1st December 2042
Nuuk, Greenland

Chapter 1

Memories, I think, are like icing sugar. Add too much water, or *time*, and the icing is thin and diluted, but add too little and it is thick and unmanageable, something you can barely stir with a spoon. My memories of David Maratse are like the icing sugar I am mixing together with Iiluuna's daughter Quaa: so thick I can barely move the spoon. I need time. Not so much that I will forget him, but just enough to spread the memories a little more evenly, thick enough to enjoy, thin enough to breathe. Quaa is watching me again, her mother's strange new friend. I should add a little more water so that I can stop crying and we can finish icing the Christmas cookies before she has to go to bed.

David's funeral was just last month, and now we have begun the darkest month of the year. We need something sweet to take the edge off the bitter night, and we need light to brighten even the darkest corners. I smile when Iiluuna lights a candle and places it on the table. I smile at Quaa, encouraging her to dip her finger in the icing. She licks the tip of her finger, and her eyes shine in the candlelight.

"It's ready," I say.

Iiluuna makes cocoa as we paint half of each cookie with a thin layer of icing sugar. I can hear her cursing the milk she burns on the bottom of the pan, and I can hear Quaa swallow as she sticks the tip of her tongue between her lips and concentrates. It's moments like these when I wish David and I had had a child. But then that chance was taken from me so many years ago. And now, so many years later, he is gone, and I have adopted the daughter he never had, and her child who he never saw. This is my family now – small and compact, manageable, my sanctuary from the streets of Nuuk.

"What are you going to do?" Iiluuna asks.

She places the cocoa in a glass jug on the table beside the candle. The light reflects and shines on the plain walls, glitters on the frosted window. There are tiny white lights hanging from the ceiling, strung from the corners on nails, draped over the light fixtures and fittings. We are elves in a grotto. We could be in the mountains, or in one of David's science fiction stories that he loved. But we are barely above street level in a city that has doubled in size since David and I moved here eleven years ago. The Chinese arrived a few years before we did and expanded the iron ore mine in the very north of *Nuup Kangerlua*, the fjord above Nuuk. They needed a town for so many Chinese workers, and they built it – Chinatown, just south of Qinngorput to the east of the city centre, together with the new harbour and airport. The first climate immigrants came next when Pipaluk Uutaaq, then minister for Housing and Infrastructure, saw an opportunity to boost Greenland's economy. The opposition parties and the media were sceptical, but when the Dutch arrived and began work on Little Amsterdam, Pipaluk was praised for her foresight, and Mitsimmavik, south of Chinatown, was transformed into a pretty colony that van Gogh would have died for. According to the media. David wasn't so sure, but we took the bus there on Saturdays when he was strong enough, stronger than his cancer, and we walked along glittered paths with granite trees cut and chipped from mountain roots. He liked the *stroopwafels*. He liked anything sweet.

"Petra?" Iiluuna says.

That's right. I must make a decision. I can only stretch my compassionate leave for so long. Not long enough.

"I could retire," I say. "David and I talked about it. I have a good pension. I have a nice apartment. I might even travel a little. Berlin, perhaps."

"You can leave it all behind?"

"Police work?"

I laugh. It is a strange sound, but it feels good.

"Yes," I say. "I can leave all that behind."

I wouldn't miss it and I have given so much of my life to the job already, so many years – from Constable to Commissioner, as a detective and a victim. Without David to come home to, I'm not sure I can cope with the street, the suffering, and the evil that lies in those dark corners without light. People think being a Police Commissioner is all about administration and politics, which it is, but a good Commissioner is never far from the street. Not in Greenland.

Without David, I think. Without him I am struggling to sleep alone in my apartment, forcing Quaa to share her mother's bed as I sleep in hers, staring at her pop posters and ornaments, waking at the beep of her new mobile phone. I laugh at the thought of how David struggled to keep up with even the most basic technological developments, at how old-fashioned people thought his books were, and how he revelled in reading them to me, his brow creased by candle-light, during winter power cuts.

"Yes," I say. "I will apply for early retirement, just as soon as I return to the office."

"When?"

I have been waiting for her to ask. It is the season of giving, but I cannot continue to just take, I can't deprive Quaa of her bed and her room any longer. I think I knew I would leave as soon as we started on the icing, the first drops of water brought the tears, as I realised that I was going home tonight, back to the apartment, to the smell and the sights that I associate with David. But not the sounds. The apartment is silent now, like the earth in which he lies, beneath the rocks and stones in one of the last reserved spots in Nuuk's city graveyard.

I take a breath and then I reach across the table to brush crusts of icing and biscuit crumbs from Quaa's cheeks.

"You can sleep in your own bed tonight," I say, as I force a smile.

Quaa's long black hair tumbles from her shoulders as she looks at her mother and I nod.

"Yes," I say. "I'm ready."

"If you're sure?"

"You've both been very kind, but it's time."

My phone buzzes and I show them the screen.

"And work calls," I say.

The intrusion is welcome, and the urgent message from the station hurries me out of Iiluuna's apartment, into my winter clothes and onto the street. They have sent a patrol car, and I climb inside, a second or two after it hums along the street and stops where the tyres have compacted the snow into a curb. Nuuk police have three of these electric SUVs, with two more arriving on the first ship in spring. They are as quiet as they are spacious. Comfortable too. I nod at the Constable behind the wheel and he pulls away from the curb.

I scan the message as he drives, teasing out the details of the text and wondering why they have called me at such a delicate time. The photos embedded in the message provide some answers, and I gasp at the sight of the banded fingers on the dead body, naked and stiff, tied with plastic ties to the railings outside the new community centre.

"Are you alright, ma'am?"

I place my mobile on my thigh, screen down, reminding myself that he is kind to ask, and that he deserves an answer.

"Have you seen the body?" I ask.

"Yes, ma'am."

"The fingers are banded," I say, and turn the screen upwards. "It might be tattoos, and if so, then…"

I sigh as he waits for me to continue. He is too young to push, but I see him glance at my bare hands.

"Yes," I say. "It's true, the backs of my fingers, between the joints, are banded with tattoos – stick and poke from a fish hook."

He would be too young to have followed the case in the media, but not so young he wouldn't have heard the stories about the Commissioner, back when she was a victim. It helps to think of that time in the third person, as if I can remove myself from the memory. But that is why they called, dragging me out of my grief only to compound it with traumatic memories. If nothing else, it makes me even more determined to retire.

The Constable parks the patrol car and escorts me to the body. The area is cordoned off, the shoppers guided around the scene by blue and white tape and gentle commands, the kind that are difficult not to understand.

"Keep moving," the police officers say. "No pictures."

Someone thought to hang a tarpaulin from the covered walkway above. It flaps with crisp crackles in the chill wind blowing between Nuuk's oldest supermarket and the entrance to the new community centre. There are people pressed to the glass of the walkway above, and I whisper to the Constable that I am fine, and perhaps he can find a colleague to clear the walkway. They have a direct view of the body, and I wonder if they can see something that the officers on the ground cannot. Perhaps I should go with the Constable, but then a deep voice and a gentle touch on my arm suggest I am wanted here. There is no escape.

"I'm sorry," Sergeant Aqqa Danielsen says, as he guides me towards the body. "It's so soon after the funeral, but when I saw the fingers, I told them to call you."

I nod as he lets go of my arm and I crouch beside the body of a young man, a Greenlander, naked and stiff in the cold, palms upwards, fingers blue and banded. It couldn't be the work of the man Aqqa and I knew, but it is plain to see that someone has been inspired by that man's work. I glance at my fingers and then search for a thin pair of gloves from the pockets of my police jacket. I pause at the touch of a length of bailing twine and the cold plastic shell of a lighter. This is not my jacket. And I remember it was one of three things I took when I left my apartment after the funeral – my phone, an overnight bag, and David's old police jacket. There are no gloves. He never used them. I tuck my hands inside the pockets, clasping the twine and the lighter like tiny talismans, and wait for Aqqa to continue his report.

"The man was strangled," he says. "We need to get the body to the morgue before we'll know more. But there's something else."

I follow Aqqa to the back of a patrol car. The swirl of blue emergency lights flash across the faces of the crowd. The Danes and the Dutch immigrants are barely indistinguishable, the Greenlanders and the Chinese more so, but mostly by the clothes they are wearing – the Chinese are layered with chicken-feathered duvet suits, loose feathers drift in the cold air above them when they move.

"This was strung around his neck," Aqqa says and hands me an advent calendar inside a large plastic evidence bag.

Father Christmas in his *Coca Cola* suit is on the front, and all but one of the windows is closed. I turn the calendar in the light.

"Today is the first of December," I say.

"*Aap.*"

"But the window that is open," I say and turn it towards Aqqa. "Is the sixteenth."

"I have no idea," he says. "But I'm pretty sure we were meant to find it. Oh, and the First Minister wants to talk to you. She's waiting in her car."

"She's here?"

Aqqa points around the patrol car and I nod as the driver of the luxurious government vehicle gets out and waves me over.

"You've finished with the scene?" I ask Aqqa.

"We were just waiting for you."

"Okay, I say. Carry on and I'll see what the First Minister wants."

The driver opens the passenger door as I walk over, and I climb inside. The interior is lit with soft lights, and Pipaluk Uutaaq looks radiant. I wonder, just for a second, what she might think of David's jacket, decorated as it is with the spots and smears of fishing and hunting adventures. She seems not to notice and offers me a drink from the cabinet beside her seat as the driver closes the door. I shake my head and wait for her to speak.

"You've seen the advent calendar?" she asks.

"Yes."

"And do you know what happens on the sixteenth of December?"

"Forgive me, First Minister. I've been a little preoccupied."

"I'm sorry. My condolences," Pipaluk says and takes my hand. "The sixteenth is the day Greenland votes for independence," she says. "You do remember?"

Despite turning off the radio, avoiding the television and the streaming media, and hiding in Iiluuna's apartment, even I cannot pretend that I don't know Greenland is set to vote, again, for independence from Denmark, again.

"We're going to get it this time," Pipaluk says. "So, you can imagine I am very concerned about the dead body in front of the community centre. It's the most central voting station in Nuuk. My father worked hard for this, she says. And we're so close."

"You think this is related?"

"Don't you?"

Pipaluk looks at me in such a way that I know all thoughts of early retirement are about to be postponed, indefinitely, at least until Greenland has cut its colonial ties.

"I want you to investigate this case personally, Commissioner."

"First Minister, with respect, I have many competent investigators. All of whom can investigate this case."

"But I want you."

"You can't tell me what to investigate, or even how I should conduct investigations," I say.

"Petra," Pipaluk says with a pat of my hand. "I just did."

Marlunngorneq

Tuesday, 2nd December 2042

Chapter 2

The apartment is as silent as I remember. I don't hear the crash and thump of the neighbour's children, nor the raised voices of the couple arguing, the distorted music of the drunk fiddling with the volume of his stereo or the sudden scream, the percussive crash, or any of the other sounds associated with apartment life in the city. All I can hear is the silence of empty space where he should be. All I can see are his books, lining the shelves – they are full of words and yet they don't speak.

Spineless.

After a moment at the door I manage to close it, but I won't remove his jacket. Not yet. I kick off my boots, but I unzip and curl the jacket around my body, pressing my fingers into the corners of the pockets, zip overlapping as I pad across the floor of the living room, ignoring the books, and pressing my face to the window, it is cool on my brow. I close my eyes. I can feel my breath against the glass, cooling; it cools my chin and my cheeks. I know the bed is made, but I haven't the strength to face it. It is after midnight, but I can't go into the bedroom.

"Just a few minutes more," I say. "Then, I promise, I will go to bed."

Tomorrow I will file for retirement. Pipaluk can find another Commissioner. If not from Nuuk, they can send a temporary replacement from Denmark, until a new one can be appointed. I don't need to do it.

Piitalaat.

I don't look around. I know it's not him. If I just press my head a little longer against the glass, if I look out across the bay and remember the view is the reason we chose to keep the apartment, even after my promotion, then he will return to the land, he will sink to rest, peacefully, beneath the snow and the rocks.

Stop it, Piitalaat.

"Stop what?" I say, as I turn around, eyes wide, searching the black corners of the room.

Let me go.

"You're the one talking."

Eeqqi, Piitalaat. It's not me.

I know it. Of course, I do.

I look at the shelves again. There are fewer books than the smallest book shelves in a Danish household, but in some parts of Greenland, in the small hunting and fishing communities, David's three shelves of science fiction books were the equivalent of the national library. And still they don't speak. Perhaps if I opened one of them, took it to bed with me, then maybe…

I let the thought hang in the air as I pull my hands out of David's deep pockets. I grab an armful of books and carry them into the bedroom, kicking the door with my heel to open it. I dump the books on the bed and return for the next shelf, and again, until his side of the bed is heavy with books. I will have to tug at the duvet to cover my body, just as I did every night, even when he was weak, and my complaints at him *hogging the duvet again* became code for *I love you* and *don't leave me*.

I take off the jacket and cover the pillow with it, crawling under the duvet in my winter salopettes and fleece. I can smell the north pressed between the fibres of his jacket as I lay my head on the pillow, and

I can feel the wind's teeth and the dogs' claws in the scratches and tears of the stiff cotton and greasy flaps covering the pockets.

Sleep, Piitalaat, he says, and I let him.

There is a practical part of my nature that takes over when it feels my emotions are getting the best of me. It's almost as if I am torn with internal jealousy. I can almost hear *practical me* sighing and shaking her head. Colleagues in the past have wondered at it, although, to be fair, there are very few police officers who haven't experienced their own *practical me* when dealing with difficult scenes and investigations. So, I'm not so special after all, and I remind myself of that as I shower, dress, and get ready to walk down the long hill from the apartment in Qinngorput to the bus stop across from the school. I could take a taxi, call for a patrol to pick me up, or even drive my own car. But today I want to see the people of Nuuk, feel them bustle and bump against my shoulders in the early morning standing-room-only bus.

I feel stronger now that I have survived the first night alone in what was *our* bed and is now my own. I have decisions to make, and that one night's sleep has given me the strength to make them.

I will go north, back to Inussuk, for a little while at least.

I should have buried him there, in the tiny graveyard on the mountainside, above the settlement. But I didn't. I will visit instead.

The short walk from the bus stop to Nuuk Police Station is just enough to colour my cheeks as I open the doors and climb the stairs to the Commissioner's office. My office. My assistant, Aron Ulloriaq stands to greet me as I hang my jacket on the rack and peel off my salopettes.

"You walked?" he asks.

"I took the bus."

Winter clothes are like a chrysalis, and as I straighten my black tie I am ready for the day.

"Is there any coffee?" I ask.

"Of course."

It is a distraction, and I almost feel guilty, but while Aron pours me a fresh mug of coffee I find the necessary paperwork in the filing cabinet by his desk. So much of our daily life is paperless, and yet some things require a formality that can be felt, as if the weight of the paper itself and the gravity pulling at it make it more important. I tuck the papers into an empty brown file and carry them into my office, slapping them on the desk as Aron brings me my morning coffee.

"What about breakfast?" he asks.

He knows I haven't eaten, and that I won't touch anything before ten o'clock. But he asks anyway, just as he has asked every morning since he started in August.

"Maybe later," I say.

He's hovering by the desk, and I am uncertain if he wants to ask about me, about the body with the banded fingers – which is also *about me*, really – or if there is something else.

"There was a call," he says. "Just before you got in. It was the doctor in the morgue."

"Dronning Ingrid's Hospital?"

"No, Kong Frederik's."

That's the new hospital, the modern one, and yet not so modern it could save David's life. I prefer to work with the staff at the old hospital. They at least don't pretend they can work miracles.

I wait for him to leave and then the light glows on the handset of my office phone. He has already patched me through. Doctor Bendt Hersholt's voice has a touch of morning grit about it, or perhaps it is late night gravel and he is annoyed at the overtime and the urgency of the dead.

"This is Commissioner Jensen," I say.

"Petra?"

I have noticed that ever since I was appointed to the post of Police Commissioner doctors prefer to use my first name, as if I have joined their ranks. Or perhaps, even after so many years, it has something to do with my sex and the reluctant acceptance of men – still – to accept that the position was something earned not rewarded.

"Doctor," I say.

"You sent me a body late last night."

"Yes."

"Cause of death was strangulation."

I want to ask why he is telling me, why not the officer assigned to the case? Sergeant Danielsen perhaps. Then I remember that the First Minister assigned me to the case. I'm sure she called the doctor too, I can hear as much in his tone of voice. He must have worked through the night.

"Anything else?" I ask.

"You saw the fingers?"

I turn the palm of my left hand upwards – trauma tattoos, a physical reminder of what I carry on the inside. David helped me heal, and *practical me* told me to get over myself and get on with life. It took a few years, but I listened, to both of them. And now I have to listen to him, the doctor, as he tells me something I already know. I'm tempted to ask him his age but bite my tongue instead. I can taste the blood as he speaks.

"The tattoos are old and crude. I think he might have done them himself."

"What's his name?" I ask.

"That's what I can't give you, not yet. We're still trying to merge the records from Dronning Ingrid's into our new system."

I let him rant for a few seconds, as I study the bands across the joints of my fingers and swallow the blood in my mouth. I close my hand around the coffee mug to hide my fingers as I rinse the blood with coffee. Right on cue, the doctor has finished, and I swallow and speak.

"You'll let me know?"

"Yes," he says.

I put the phone down when I hear him take a breath. I'm not normally so rude, but I can see Aron hovering at the door. Sergeant Danielsen is behind him.

"Come in," I say.

"We've got another one," Danielsen says.

He steps into my office and shows me the screen of his mobile. The body is charred as if it has been burned. He swipes the next photo onto the screen and shows me the advent calendar. It is identical to the first, and the window for the ninth day of December is open.

"Have we got forensics on this?" I ask.

"They are at the scene."

"Take me there," I say.

Danielsen has a *new-car* grin and he wears it well. He owns the driver's seat, filling it with a middle-aged stomach and backside that could be the result of patrol snacks or home cooking. I have met his wife, the lovely Kuuka, and I imagine it is a bit of both. The SUV purrs along the snow-packed road and I almost wish we could just keep driving. The roads in Nuuk have expanded with the city, there is even a bridge spanning *Kangerluarsunnguaq Fjord*, east of the city, providing access to the United States Coast Guard Station Nuuk. An imaginative name for a high-security foreign base. No-one travels across the bridge because the Americans won't let them. They prefer to remain secluded and secretive, just one of the conditions for their substantial contribution to the new harbour. They won't be visiting anytime soon, and neither will we.

And just like that, the journey is over, and so too are my plans for early retirement, as soon as I see the body. Practical me steps aside for my emotions as I see what I failed to notice in Danielsen's photograph – the charred body is too small for an adult.

This part of Nuuk has escaped the developer's eye. The concrete walls of the courtyard and the apartments above are fatigued, like the occupants. I can feel the chill wind press and flap the fabric of my trousers as it blows from the road, swirling snow over my boots, and dusting the black with a layer of fine white sugar. I should have worn my salopettes. I thought this would be a quick visit to the crime scene, before I told Danielsen to carry on, and then returned to the office. I know Aron has a backlog of paperwork for me to see to but is too polite to say so.

I crouch beside the body, see the charred remains of a wooden chair and the streak of black that has burned through the snow from an empty fuel can.

"We're not sure if it is a child or someone very small."

"Look at the size of the hands," I say. "And the head."

Practical me is back, and I'm almost embarrassed. But years of police work attune the eye to some things that others might not see, at least not to begin with. Someone was burned to death – a child or a small adult – and the papers and streaming media have another body to report.

"Show me the advent calendar."

Danielsen taps one of the technicians on the shoulder and they fetch the calendar from the van. The technician's eyes are obscured by the mask, and his or her clothes are hidden beneath protective overalls. I can't tell if it is a man or a woman, but the eyes, what I can see of them, are all business. I nod my thanks and turn the calendar in my hands.

It is a duplicate of the first, and I imagine there will be more. Twenty-four in all, if that's what this is – the first two murders in a series. But if the open windows on the advent calendar are significant then they need to be studied, and the other windows need to be opened. I press the calendar into Danielsen's hands.

"Congratulations, Aqqa," I say. "You're the lead investigator."

"But the First Minister…"

"Does not decide how we work. I'll stay close, but I won't get in your way. Oh, and you'll need a task force. Any thoughts?"

"Atii Napa is just back from leave."

"Good. Call her. Get her up to speed as soon as you get back to the station."

"You don't want a ride?"

"No," I say. "I'm still officially on leave. I'll make some calls, from home and assemble the team. I want everything ready by first thing tomorrow morning. I'll see you then."

Pingasunngorneq

Wednesday, 3rd December 2042

Chapter 3

I waited until they were settled, and Aron had finished handing out the breakfast rolls. It was one of those moments when, from a distance, one might worry that the tone was too light and cheery for a murder investigation. The collegial small talk while buttering rolls, or the humorous jibes that inevitably follow a small mistake, or perhaps even a romantic rebuff from the weekend. But it is these small inappropriate things that make the difference when working within and for the community, from the inside, often isolated like the Americans on the base across the fjord.

I let them chatter a few minutes more as I observe the team Danielsen has put together. There is Atii Napa, bronzed and beaming from her short break in Greece. She is two years younger than me, but one could be forgiven for thinking it wasn't at least ten. I think of my old colleague and friend Gaba Alatak and smile at the image of him running his own company and getting the boys ready for school while Atii, his wife and former patrol partner, cruise the streets at night in one of the new SUVs. She was ready to cancel her trip to Greece with her sister when she heard about David's death. I'm not sure she has forgiven me for ordering her to go on holiday, but it was the right thing to do. David wouldn't have wanted the fuss.

I don't know the man sitting next to her, but I have read his file, and can understand why Danielsen wanted him on the task force. Ooqi Kleemann is from Upernavik, and I know David would have liked him. He has the quiet smile of shy intelligence that you often see in the smaller towns and villages. His glasses are thick, and I wonder if it is because he has spent more time in front of a computer screen than he has on the ice? His file says he is an IT specialist, and the attached notes show a record of pre-teen hacking that was expunged prior to him starting high school. Someone is looking out for Ooqi, and I decide that I will do the same.

Expunged.

I'm lost in the word for a moment, until Danielsen coughs and beckons me to the front of the room. I said he was the lead investigator, but he seems reluctant to start. A quick look over my shoulder suggests why, and I present my best thin-lipped smile to Greenland's First Minister.

"Don't mind me," she says.

But we do mind, and I whisper to Aron to find her a chair, as I walk to the front of the room. I amend my opening speech for her benefit and begin.

"Thank you, Aqqa," I say, as he sits down. "You're a small team, but you've got the full weight and cooperation of the department behind you. It's true; we're still short-staffed. We needed more police officers before the Chinese arrived, fourteen years ago, and we still needed them when the first Dutch immigrants began work on Little Amsterdam. I expect to reach out to the Chinese and Dutch security staff after this meeting, but I just wanted to get you started, and to hand over to Aqqa. He'll walk you through what we know."

"I thought you were leading the investigation?" Pipaluk says from her seat behind the task force. "That was what we agreed, Commissioner."

The image of her father, the late Malik Uutaaq,

flickers through my mind as I return the look she casts from the back of the room. He was a popular figure in Greenlandic politics, but he must have loaded his genes with power and persuasion when he created her. She is twice the politician he was, and twice as popular. He helped sow the original seeds for Greenlandic independence, but she has nurtured them, and soon, according to the opinion polls, they will bear fruit.

"I will be monitoring progress on a daily basis," I say.

"Closely?"

"Very."

"And who will report to me?"

"I will," I say, as I move to lean against the wall.

Danielsen takes his cue, rises from his seat, and turns to face the small task force, while I work on *expunging* the last few minutes from my mind.

He really has put on weight, I think, as Danielsen runs through what we know of the two murders. It helps, I realise, to think about such things, and to be back at work again. The problem with the new pay system that Aron told me about this morning, the dead battery in the newest SUV, Aqqa's gut, and the crime scene photos he flashes onto the wall all help to push thoughts of David to some quiet part of my mind. I can revisit them later, as I did last night when the weight of David's books fooled me into thinking he really was hogging the duvet.

Piitalaat.

"What?"

Focus.

"Do you have anything to add?" Danielsen asks.

"Remind me again."

"We're waiting for a positive identification of the victims, and we were talking about the calendar. The sixteenth is the referendum," he says with a nod towards the back of the room. "But we've got nothing on the ninth."

"That's not completely true," Atii says and stands up.

Danielsen moves to one side as she casts a file from her mobile to the wall screen with a flick of her finger. Atii slips her finger and thumb inside two thimbles, clicking them together to highlight boxes of text on the screen, and pointing with the laser bead embedded in the thimble on her finger. I smile at the memory of the day I told David we were getting digital thimbles on trial.

Focus, he says, and I send him a mental roll of the eyes. Although, it is nice to be working with him again. I catch myself and process the thought as Atii runs through a few associations with the number nine.

"According to Norse Mythology, there are nine worlds connected by the world tree Yggdrasil. Odin hung from the tree for nine days before he gained knowledge of the runes."

"You're looking at myths?" Pipaluk says.

"We're looking at links," Atii says. "Anything."

"Keep going, Atii," I say.

"Odin and Yggdrasil might be relevant if the suspect is a Dane, but the Chinese have a lot more nines in their culture, mostly associated with the dragon, its nine forms, and nine children. The number nine is lucky in Chinese culture."

"And do we have any Chinese festivals coming up?"

"*Aap*," Atii says. "Dongzhi is the Chinese celebration of the Winter Solstice."

"When is it?" I ask.

"The twenty-third of December."

"*Lillejuleaften*," I say, remembering the Danish term for the night before Christmas Eve. If I remember correctly, that was a night to be celebrated because all the preparations for Christmas Eve should have been completed, the last presents bought and wrapped, food and last-minute decorations ticked off the list. "That might be something. But I'll call the Chinese as soon as we're done."

"There's one more thing," Atii says with a look at Danielsen. At a nod from him she continues. "The ninth letter of the alphabet is *I*."

I wait as Atii glances at Danielsen.

"The sixteenth letter is *P*," she says.

"I'm listening," I say, as my stomach grows heavy and cold.

"The bands on your fingers," Danielsen says. "I'm sorry, Commissioner, but I was there. I remember."

And so do I.

"That's why I called you. I knew you were still on leave, but…"

"It's okay, Aqqa," I say. "Please, continue."

"The tattoos on your fingers are the same as the dead body from the community centre. The First Minister thinks the sixteenth window has something to do with the referendum, and she might be right, but *P* is the first letter in your name."

"But the second is *E*," Pipaluk says. "The Commissioner's name is *Petra*."

"That's not what Maratse called her," Danielsen

says.

He catches my eye and I nod that I'm okay.

"What?"

"David called me *Piitalaat*," I say. "It's the Greenlandic spelling of my name."

"It's just a theory," Danielsen says. "We don't have a lot to work on at the moment."

"But if you're right," I say. "Then it's personal."

"Yes, ma'am."

"Alright." I walk past Danielsen and Atii to the wall. The glare from the screen is warm on my skin as I breathe, slowly, knowing what I have to do. "Ooqi," I say, as I turn around. "Danielsen has chosen you as the tech specialist. Is that right?"

He nods.

"Then I'm giving you permission to open the old files. You'll need a codeword clearance for some of them. Or not," I say and frown at the colour rising in Ooqi's cheeks.

"When I saw the tattooed fingers," Danielsen says, "I asked Ooqi to see what he could find." Danielsen shrugs. "He's pretty good, ma'am."

"That's why he's on the team," I say and smile at Ooqi. His cheeks flame and I find that despite the personal nature of the task force's theory, I almost feel sorry for him. "I'll be in my office," I say, as I excuse myself.

Pipaluk glares at me as I walk out of the room, and I can still feel her eyes on my back as I enter my office. It must be ten o'clock, I realise, when I see the buttered roll on a plate on my desk. I'm not hungry, but Aron will know if I don't eat. I take a bite and wash it down with a swallow of fresh coffee. I buzz for him to come in as I sit down behind my desk.

"I need to call the Chinese," I say. "What was the name of their security liaison?"

"Tan Yazhu," Aron says. "Yazhu is his first name."

I frown at the nagging thought that the name is new to me.

"He arrived shortly before the funeral," Aron says. "He is the new liaison."

"What happened to the last one?"

"Recalled," Aron says and shrugs. "We never met that one either."

"Well, see if you can put me through to Tan Yazhu. I'll take it here."

I pick up the phone a few seconds later but am distracted by the new position of the folder containing my retirement papers. A quick glance through the glass wall of my office at Aron's desk reveals nothing. Perhaps he looked. Perhaps he didn't. I might ask him later, but the voice on the other end of the line pulls me back into the investigation.

"Tan Yazhu?"

"*Shì.*"

"This is Commissioner Jensen, from Nuuk Police."

"*Shì.*"

He sounds distracted and I wonder if I have caught him in a meeting.

"I'd like to meet with you, as soon as possible."

"We can meet," he says. "But not right now."

"Are you alright?" I ask.

"You say you are police?"

"That's right."

"Then maybe you should come. We have found a body."

"Where are you?"

"Chinatown, of course. Apartment nine…"

I don't hear the rest, and I will have to call him back as I let the phone slip from my ear. It could be a coincidence, but if Atii and Danielsen's theory is to gain traction it needed another number, and a second number nine provides the third letter *I* of my name.

Piitalaat.

"Ma'am?" Aron says, as he enters my office.

"Yes?"

"I've just talked with the Chinese Liaison. Tan Yazhu?"

"Yes."

"He said you were talking, but that you were cut off." Aron walks around the desk and takes the handset gently from my hand. "I've sent a patrol car," he says. "And Danielsen."

"That's good, Aron."

"Are you sure you're alright? You're very pale."

"I'll be fine," I say, as I stand up. "I just need a minute."

I run a basin of cold water in the washroom. The bands on my fingers are refracted as I plunge my hands into the water. I try to lift them to my face, to clear my mind, but they don't move. I don't know how long I have been standing there, but it is Atii's face beside mine in the mirror.

"You've got a lovely tan," I say, as she smiles and smooths my hair from my cheeks.

"Gaba says you should come for dinner."

"That's nice," I say. "Soon. Maybe."

"Are you alright?"

"Yes, of course," I say.

She steps back as I force my hands to my face

and wash the tears from my cheeks.

Sisamanngorneq

Thursday, 4th December 2042

Chapter 4

The books weighing down the duvet are not heavy enough and I can't sleep, neither am I alone. I know there is a patrol car parked outside, special duty, something Danielsen arranged with the Deputy Police Commissioner. *He* might be on a course in Copenhagen, but Danielsen must have briefed him and requested the security detail. I think it's an overreaction, of course, but Danielsen is right about the links to my past. I think about this as I dress and leave the apartment, startling the police officer in one of the older Toyota's when I knock on the window.

"Let's go for a ride," I say, as I open the passenger door and settle in beside him. The car is cramped and familiar compared to the new electric models.

"Yes, ma'am." He starts the engine; it coughs and splutters in the cold. "Where to?"

"Downtown."

The tyres squeal in the snow as we pull out of the car park by my apartment in Qinngorput. The air has sunk inside the wheels with the cold and it takes a kilometre to warm it up. The *thud thud thud* of the triangular wheels smooths into a regular rumble by the time we reach the first roundabout.

"What's your name?" I ask.

"Nikolaj Valkyrien," he says.

Valkyrien. The name is familiar, and I try to remember where I have heard it before as we drive past the five-pointed paper Christmas stars lit by soft bulbs in the windows of the apartments – almost every apartment – on the way into town. There are no Northern Lights in the sky tonight, and the cloud is heavy with snow. Nikolaj turns up the heat as we head up Nuuk's main street *Aqqusinersuaq*, past Hotel Hans Egede, now fifty-three years old. *Just three years older than me*, I think. But that wasn't what I was trying to remember.

"Your mother was a police woman?"

"Yes," he says. "In Denmark."

"What is her name?"

"Ada."

"That's right. I remember now."

"Did you meet her?"

"Once. She helped a friend of mine."

Nikolaj says nothing more and I don't pry as we slow by the new housing and office development area overlooking the fjord at the southern tip of the city. The office windows of the Nuuk Media Group are lit and there is activity beneath the bright lights behind the Christmas stars. Nikolaj slows as I point at the car park.

"I'll be about an hour," I say, as I get out of the car.

Nikolaj follows me inside the building, hovering a respectful distance behind me as I sign in with the Âmo Security Guard. The uniform is familiar, and the guard catches me staring at the logo on the patch on his arm.

"It's Âmo, the shaman's familiar," he says, as I frown at the creature in the logo. The head is massive, and the long arms wrap around the company name. "The boss makes sure we know. It's part of the training."

"Your boss?"

"Gaba Alatak."

Of course. I should remember. It's almost as if

my memory has been shattered since David's death and I am gathering the pieces, turning and fitting them in my mind each day, rebuilding my memory and clearing my vision. I'm not sure I am fit for duty, not yet. I wonder if I will ever be.

But I do remember the day Gaba saw an opportunity to create a private security company when the government announced that the first Chinese workers would be arriving within the year. Fourteen years ago. Gaba left the police a few months later, took out a loan and started recruitment for Greenland Private Security. I had forgotten when and why he had changed the name – something about being more Greenlandic, perhaps. I would have to ask him the next time we saw each other.

"Is Qitu Kalia in the building?" I ask.

"He's in his office. They're putting the paper to bed," he says. "Digitally. Qitu never leaves until all the top stories are ready." The guard grinned. "He sleeps here a lot."

"Can you let him know I'm on my way up?"

The guard nods and waves us through the security entrance. It must be Nikolaj's first time at Nuuk Media Group and I watch as he admires the thick glass, cameras and heavy locking mechanisms on the inner door.

"Qitu has a reputation for exposing powerful people and underground movements," I say, as the guard buzzes us into the building. "Is this your first time in Nuuk?"

"My first time in Greenland," Nikolaj says. "I'm covering someone's maternity leave."

"Right," I say, as I wonder who it might be. I really have lost touch, although, to be fair, the department is twice the size it once was when I was a Sergeant.

Qitu meets us outside the elevator. His hug is tight like the arms of the shaman's familiar, protective and sincere. I step back when he lets go so that he can read my lips – he stopped using hearing aids a long time ago. *That* I do remember.

"You're busy," I say, and gesture at the journalists hunched over their desks.

"We're working on *The Calendar Man*," he says. "It's big news, Petra."

"I wish it wasn't." I can feel my brow knitting. "How do you know it's a man?"

"It's an educated guess. We don't have all the answers, just a lot of questions. But that's why you're here."

I nod and gesture towards his office. "Can we talk?"

"Sure."

"I'll be a little while," I say to Nikolaj. "I'll find you in the canteen when I'm done."

I wait for Nikolaj to nod, pointing him in the direction of the canteen before following Qitu to his office. I realise now why he chooses not to wear his hearing aids, even with computers and soft keypads, the noise and chatter between the desks is overwhelming. I relax once we are inside his office. The door closes with a soft hermetic sigh. Qitu pours coffee and we sit in the comfy chairs around a small table in the corner of his office, a few metres from the clutter of his desk.

"You've seen the similarities," I say, choosing to launch straight into the details of the case I wish didn't exist.

"Your tattoos," Qitu says, as he glances at my fingers.

"And the calendar windows," I say. "The three dates match the letters of my name."

"Three?"

"Three numbers." I pause for a moment as I consider my history with Qitu, and how much I should reveal at this moment. I trust him, I realise, and then the decision is made. "There was a body found in Chinatown last night. No calendar, but the apartment number was number nine. Danielsen found fake snow sprayed around the number, dashed with the victim's blood." Qitu reaches for the notepad on the table and I stop him with a shake of my head. "Please, let us release a statement first," I say.

"Okay," he says. "And the third number would be?"

"Another *I*. So, now we have *PII*."

"Piitalaat," he says, and for a second, I think it is David's voice. They both have such soft voices.

"It's a theory. And that's why I'm here, Qitu. Who would know about me? I don't remember you writing about me in your article."

"I never mentioned you," he says.

"And the man who did this is dead," I say, as I look at my palms.

"*Aap.*"

"Pipaluk thinks it's a scare tactic, to keep people indoors and stop them voting on the sixteenth. What do you think?"

"I think she could be right, but…"

"Qitu?"

"If your theory is right."

"Danielsen and Atii's theory," I say.

"If they are right, then it could have more to do with you, and maybe Maratse."

"David is gone. This can't have anything to do with him. And the scare tactics seem plausible. What we don't yet know is the identity of the victims. The young man with the banded fingers has yet to be identified, and the charred body of the small person – perhaps a dwarf – is proving difficult. They are looking at dental records, but you know the history of dentistry in Greenland. They still have problems recruiting dentists in the smaller towns and settlements. We might never find any records."

"And the third victim?"

"Chinese. We're waiting to hear more. But then, if we ignore the number on the door, there doesn't seem to be any connection. Although, we know that nine is a lucky number in China."

"Not for the victim," Qitu says.

"No. I suppose not."

The coffee is cooling in the mug and I force myself to take a sip as my mind whirls with possible links and connections.

"I have another number for you," Qitu says with a smile.

"What's that?"

"Today is December the 4th. It's the one hundred and eleventh anniversary of the first screening of Boris Karloff's *Frankenstein*. They're showing it tonight at the cinema. We should go."

"A horror movie?"

"From the 1930s, Petra." Qitu laughs. "You need a distraction, and it's science fiction. David would have gone."

"He read books, Qitu. He didn't watch movies."

"Only because he didn't have a television. Come with me. It will be good to get out."

"I am out," I say.

"Before breakfast. It doesn't mean you are *out*, it just means you can't sleep. Why don't you call in sick? Go home and rest. I'll pick you up later."

"I'm the Commissioner, Qitu. I can't call in sick."

"You're still on compassionate leave. Aren't you?"

"You've been talking to Danielsen."

"*Aap*. And he tells me he has a task force now. Take the day. I will pick you up, and we can watch the movie."

"I'm not sure, Qitu. A horror movie?"

"It's a classic. Lots of overacting. I'll buy the popcorn."

"Popcorn?"

"Definitely."

"Fine," I say. "But we will need three tickets." I nod in the direction of the canteen. "I have a chaperone. Danielsen's orders."

I think about cancelling at least three times during the day, but Qitu has conveniently turned his phone off. I give up, and concentrate on relaxing, showering, and tugging on a pair of jeans and a baggy sweater. Nikolaj is in plain clothes when I meet him at the door, just as Qitu arrives in his Tesla SUV.

The cinema is almost empty, but Qitu spots someone he thinks I should meet as we carry our popcorn from the counter to our seats.

"This is Geert Aalders," he says in English, as he introduces me to a short man with a finely-trimmed beard. "He was the one who told me about this special screening of *Frankenstein*."

"It's just possible I gave the cinema manager a tip, in the hope he might show one of my favourite films," Geert says. "It's far too festive for my liking."

"You don't like Christmas?" I ask.

"I think it's possible to overdose." He laughs. "However, tomorrow is *Sinterklaas*. I'm excited about that."

"You're Dutch?"

"You didn't guess?" Geert smiles. "It's alright; there are lots of foreigners in Nuuk these days. But some of us live here now. I am assistant to the Jonkheer, Coenraad Kuijpers. I think your Sergeant has scheduled a meeting for tomorrow morning." He leans closer for a second and lowers his voice. "We're quite concerned about the murders."

"I meant to call yesterday," I say. "But something came up."

"Yes," he says. "We heard about the body in Chinatown."

"Come on," Qitu says. "Let's find our seats, enjoy the movie."

I watch as the monster is winched up into the electrical storm and lowered again to the laboratory floor. The doctor's passion is alarming, and I wonder what David would have thought about it. I see that Nikolaj is watching me, while Qitu and his Dutch friend are mesmerised by the black and white drama playing out on the screen.

"Do you want to go, ma'am?" Nikolaj says.

I nod and follow him out of the cinema. Reanimation is perhaps too strong a subject for someone who has just buried a loved one, and the young constable recognised what the film buffs did not.

"Thank you," I say.

I am about to suggest coffee in the café while we wait for Qitu, but my mobile buzzes in my pocket and I recognise Danielsen's number.

"Aqqa," I say, as I answer it.

"Where are you?"

"With Frankenstein's monster." I laugh.

"Then you know?" he says.

The undertone in his voice suggests I have made an inappropriate joke.

"Know what?"

"We had a call from the morgue. Someone has taken parts of the victim's bodies."

Tallimanngorneq

Friday, 5th December 2042

Chapter 5

"I want more officers on the street," Pipaluk says, as she walks into my office. "And I want you to put a muzzle on Qitu Kalia." She snaps the paper edition of *Oqaasaq*, the Nuuk Media Group's expensive and limited print edition of its online newspaper. I think the Lapland rosebay flower logo is pretty, and a perfect choice for a newspaper that investigates important issues concerning Greenland and its people. Of course, there are times when I wish it didn't; now being one of them.

"I can't spare any more officers."

"Give them overtime."

"On what budget?"

"Yours, of course," she says.

"That's a problem," I say. "Until Greenland is officially independent of Denmark, the Police will continue to fall under Danish administration. The budget is decided in Denmark…"

"Based on your recommendations."

"Yes, to a degree."

"Surely you can demand more money when situations demand more resources?"

"If it was only about the money," I say. "But I only have so many officers. They can't work twenty-four-hour shifts. Most of them have families. And there are a lot of married couples within the department." I stand up and knock on the window, cupping an imaginary mug of coffee to my lips when Aron looks up from his desk. "First Minister," I say, and gesture to one of the chairs around the table. "Perhaps we can find another solution."

"Body parts were removed from the morgue,

Commissioner," she says, as she sits down. "I want a police officer on the door to the morgue."

"There are better things – more urgent things – for a police officer to do than guard the morgue," I say. "Besides, the hospital should have a security budget. They could use Gaba's company."

"Âmo? We have them in the parliament building."

"Exactly. Now, if you were to suggest to the hospital administration that they beef up their security, perhaps we can avoid another incident like this one."

"And Qitu? According to his paper, The Calendar Man is building Frankenstein's monster."

It is a sensational headline, and a far cry from Nuuk Media Group's investigative background.

"It sells papers and subscriptions," I say.

"And frightens people off the street."

Pipaluk waits as Aron places coffee and buttered rolls on the table. It must be ten o'clock, already. I take a roll as Pipaluk adds milk and sugar to her coffee.

"I share your concern, First Minister, but I can't spare any more officers. I simply don't have them, even if I could pay them. But, if you're concerned…"

"Aren't you?"

"Yes, of course. I'm just saying that you could talk to Gaba, and maybe find the resources to put his security guards in key places. It would make the people feel safer. In the meantime, I can increase the frequency of patrols, and make the police officers I have more visible."

"You should have done that already."

She's right. Perhaps I would have if I was

thinking straight.

"It's only been four days," I say. "We are reacting, and already have a task force in place. There's only so much we can do, until we catch a break, as they say."

I relax as Pipaluk's shoulders sag and she leans back in her chair. Aron appears at the door and I wave him in.

"The Jonkheer has arrived," he says.

"Would you like to sit in on the meeting, First Minister?" I say.

"You're going to talk about security?"

"I'm sure that's his main focus, yes."

"Then I'll stay."

"More coffee, Aron," I say, as I stand up to greet the Jonkheer of Little Amsterdam.

I recognise Geert Aalders as he walks behind the taller and better dressed Jonkheer. Coenraad Kuijpers is older than me, but not yet sixty. He is taller than most of the Greenlanders I know, with the exception of Gaba. The Jonkheer's handshake is firm, warm and dry. *A little too dry*, I think, as I notice the pink rash of eczema on his knuckles.

"It's the cold," he says, when he sees me look at his hands.

"You'll get used to it."

"I suppose we will." He steps to one side to let Geert into the office. "You've met my assistant?"

"Yes, last night," I say. "Shall we sit at the table?"

I wait as Pipaluk stands up to shake the hands of the Dutchmen and Aron brings more coffee. Geert is the first to sit. He pulls a small tablet out of his pocket and opens a new page for notes.

"Do we say Merry Christmas?" I ask.

"Ah, *Sinterklaas*," the Jonkheer says and smiles. "I'm impressed."

"Don't be. Geert mentioned it last night. I imagine that's why you want to meet today."

"Yes, we're concerned about the situation. This *Calendar Man*, it's not pleasant and we are worried." He pours a cup of coffee. "There are roughly three thousand Dutch citizens in Mitsimmavik, or *Little Amsterdam* as you call it. We have a small local constabulary, as approved under the initial agreement with your government," he says and looks at Pipaluk, "and brokered with Anna Riis from the Danish government. I think we have ten officers in total."

"Eight," Geert says. "Two of them are away on training at the moment in the Netherlands."

"So, not many," the Jonkheer says. I believe the Chinese have their own security measures. Is that right?"

"Yes," I say. "Although, their numbers are more fluid as they change with the number of workers they have at any one time. I think they have thirty security personnel at the mine, and fifteen in Chinatown."

"*Chinatown*," he says.

His eyes glitter in the light and I decide that I like this Jonkheer better than the first one.

"Greenland is a big country," I say, "but we have very few people. When the city expanded, and we got our own Chinatown and Little Amsterdam, it made Nuuk feel like New York."

"Just colder," he says.

"Yes."

I notice that Pipaluk has little to say, and I wonder if I have missed something. She seems to struggle to look at the Jonkheer and avoids looking at

Geert altogether. I should remember the details about the agreement, but like a lot of things since David's death, I have a lot of pieces of the puzzle, but need to put them back together again to make sense of them. It feels like the ice forming on the sea, small plates and pancakes fusing as the water temperature drops, drifting apart with the warmer winds, and then merging and freezing to create a solid, tangible whole. At least, that was how it once was further north when we lived in Inussuk, but now the ice is less certain. Climate change hasn't just affected the Dutch, the whole world has had to adapt to changing environments, new threats and new opportunities.

"We have a small celebration this evening, in the administration building," the Jonkheer says. "We want our people – all the people in Nuuk – to feel safe, and I want to ask if you will be increasing your patrols this evening?"

I struggle for a moment to remember what we did last year, and the Jonkheer sees it.

"Last year was different," he says.

"Yes, it was."

"Perhaps you can send a couple of officers to the celebration. It will be entertaining for them and reassuring for us."

"And a few extra patrols during the night," Geert says. "It would be useful to know where they will be and at what time so that we can coordinate with our own constabulary."

I glance at Pipaluk, anticipating her reaction when I agree to double the patrols in Little Amsterdam tonight, but she excuses herself to answer a call on her mobile.

"I'll have my watch officer contact your

constabulary," I say.

"*Hartelijk bedankt*," the Jonkheer says, and I can see that he means it. "And perhaps you will come too? It will be a very pleasant evening, I am sure."

"Of course," I say.

I think of Nikolaj as the Dutch prepare to leave, and hope that he is sleeping as it seems we are going out again this evening.

"If there is anything we can do to help," the Jonkheer says, as he steps into the corridor. "You only have to ask."

"And I will," I say.

I watch them leave and then sit down at my desk. Aron clears away the coffee and rolls. He hovers at the door, hands full of plates and cups, and an apologetic look on his face.

"Aron?"

"I just wanted to say I'm sorry."

"About what?"

"I thought it was something that I needed to file," he says. He nods at the folder on my desk. "I haven't told anyone."

"And I haven't signed it yet," I say.

"It's not my place, ma'am, but I would hate to see you go."

"I appreciate that, Aron. Thank you."

His cheeks regain some of their colour and I smile again.

"There's something else, isn't there," I say, as he seems reluctant to leave.

"There's a man outside. I said you were busy, but he said he would wait. I couldn't get rid of him."

"You tried?"

"He's pretty big for a Greenlander."

I only know one *big* Greenlander, tall, powerful, confident and arrogant. Aron couldn't know that the big Greenlander waiting to see me is an ex-cop and an ex-lover.

"Send him in," I say, as I try to not to smile.

The cups rattle in Aron's hands as he calls to the man.

"Do you want me to stay?" he asks.

The cups rattle for a second time in tune to the heavy footfalls landing on the floor of the corridor outside my office.

"If you think it's best," I say, and then I laugh as Aron shrinks against the door to make room for Gaba Alatak. The image is priceless, and my cheeks ache as he enters the room.

"Gaba," I say, as I walk around my desk and wrap my arms around him. He hugs back, resting his head on top of mine. I can feel the muscles barely contained inside the sleeves of his jacket, and I hear the muffled rattle of cups as Aron leaves the office and closes the door.

"He's new," Gaba says.

"And very young," I say, as I press my hand on Gaba's cheek, smiling at the white stubble outnumbering the black. "I'm pleased you came."

"Atii said you were back at work. I would have come sooner, but I've been busy, and the boys are…"

"Gorgeous. I've seen pictures."

"I was going to say frustrating. Miki has just discovered girls. He's never home."

"Were you any different?"

"Probably not." Gaba pulls out a chair and sits at the table. "You disappeared after the funeral."

"I know," I say, as I sit down. "I met a woman at

the funeral. David helped her when she was a child. I kind of moved in with them for a few days. Silly really, but I felt closer to him when I was with them."

"It's not silly if it makes you feel better."

"I could have called," I say.

"You don't have to do anything. Only when you're ready. I'm surprised you're back so early. It's The Calendar Man, isn't it? Atii told me about…"

"The tattoos?"

"And her theory." Gaba taps the table with a thick knuckle. "What are you doing about protection?"

"I've got Nikolaj.

"Who's he? Do I know him?"

"He's a constable from Denmark. Danielsen arranged it."

"Where is he now?" Gaba says and makes a display of turning his thick bald head to scan the room. "I don't see him, Petra."

"He's sleeping, probably. He's been sitting in a patrol car outside my apartment the last two nights."

"Not good enough."

"Gaba," I say and reach for his hand. "You're sweet. You always have been, but it's not your job to protect me. It wasn't then, and it isn't now."

He grips my hand and looks away. I squeeze his fingers as he starts to tremble.

"I almost lost you once," he says. "It won't happen again." He looks at me and I can see the energy in his eyes, can almost feel the heat. "I can't let it happen again. I promised Maratse."

"I know."

Gaba lets go of my hand and pushes his chair back. "Eat with us tonight," he says, as he stands up.

"Bring this Nikolaj."

"So, you can vet him?"

"Sure," he says.

"You're impossible."

"*Aap*. That's my job. Speaking of which," he says and looks at his watch. "I have a meeting with the First Minister."

"Well, you'd better go," I say. "But I can't come tonight. I've been invited to *Sinterklaas* in Little Amsterdam. It's a Christmas celebration," I say, as Gaba frowns.

"Lots of people? I don't like it."

"You don't have to like it. I'm going, and I have Nikolaj with me, plus the extra patrols we're adding to the night shift."

I stand up to give Gaba a last hug, only to pause when Danielsen appears at the door. He is out of breath, and I wonder if it is the stairs or the reason he needs to see me. I realise it could be both.

"Gaba," he says, with a nod. "I need to speak to the Commissioner."

"I was just leaving," Gaba says. He squeezes my hand as he leaves.

"What is it, Aqqa?"

"*Sinterklaas* has been cancelled," he says.

"That was fast. Why?"

"They found the missing body parts," Danielsen says and takes a breath. "They were stitched to a fourth body and left on a chair inside the Dutch administration building. Atii is there now. I came to tell you."

"Alright," I say. "Let's go."

"*Naamik*," he says shakes his head. "I've called Nikolaj. You're going home."

I almost laugh, but I can see that he is serious.

"I don't think you can make that decision, Sergeant."

"Probably not, but, officially, you are on compassionate leave until Monday. The Deputy Commissioner gave me explicit instructions to make sure you stay at home this weekend."

"Aqqa, are you putting me under house arrest?"

"If I have to, ma'am," he says.

Arfininngorneq

Saturday, 6th December 2042

Sinterklaas

Chapter 6

Danielsen said nothing about finding an advent calendar on the Frankenstein victim and it bothers me as I lie under one half of the duvet and pretend that the weight of the books tugging the other half is David. I should get up, and my curiosity about the case finally pulls me out of bed and I put on a pot of coffee. It is dark outside. It won't be light before mid-morning, and I can see Nikolaj's patrol car pulling out of the parking area. He stops beside the day shift and I get a sudden shiver of guilt as I realise I didn't think about Nikolaj sitting in the cold through the night. His relief has one of the new SUVs and I wonder if it is warmer than the older Toyota.

I carry my coffee to my desk and open the computer with a few curt voice commands, followed by an iris-check to access the secure department server. I open the task force folder and decide to start with the first victim, the one linked with my own past. The notes attached to the file indicate that he is still unidentified. I fetch more coffee from the kitchen, pull thick woollen socks over my feet, and David's old police jacket around my shoulders. There is a faint smell of fish and dog from the jacket as I work my way through the first victim's file.

I concentrate on the bands between the joints of the victim's fingers. They are like my own, but the ink is lighter, or perhaps it is the contrast in the photograph. I press my nose into the shoulder of David's jacket, drawing in the strength to dig deep and recall what I know of the bands on my fingers. I can see that Ooqi has merged my file with the first victim's and I nod at the highlighted reference to the *loyalty card* as each band represented an act, and once the fingers were full of bands the person was rewarded. In my case and the case of a young man called Salik Erngsen from Uummannaq in the north, freedom was the promised reward. I was rescued. Salik was murdered. But we were both freed, from *him*. As far as I knew, I was the only survivor.

The man's fingers provide a link that suggests someone knows what happened to Salik and me twenty-four years ago. Alternatively, the young man found dead outside the community centre has links to my past, but the killer doesn't. the computer mistakes my sigh of frustration as a command, and I have to scroll back down the page to Atii's follow-up notes and an additional photograph. The young man's lower left leg and foot, together with his right forearm have been removed. There is a second photograph of a bloody bone saw on the metal gurney beside the victim. I look at my arm and my leg and wonder if the thief carried them off in a sports bag, a backpack or a shopping bag. An additional note from Atii spoils any hope of finding out if the thief was caught on camera – the firmware for the security cameras was being updated on the night of the 4th December.

Now, is that a coincidence? Is it convenient, or was it contrived? Either way the thief or the killer, likely one and the same, had access to the security system, or knowledge of the update. A quick check of Atii's notes confirms that she has considered the same thing and a profile of the so-called *Calendar Man* is emerging.

He or she works in hospital security, works for the security contractors, or knows someone who has access to the camera systems.

And, it's possible, I think, *that he knows about me.*

Another note reveals that the contractor for the cameras is based in Nuuk and that Atii has pinned a meeting in her activity log.

"Why didn't she send Ooqi? He's the tech guy." I wonder, and the computer beeps and flashes a window that suggests I rephrase the question. "Never mind," I say, and take a sip of coffee. A text message scrolls across the screen as I swallow.

CAN I HELP YOU, MA'AM?

"Ooqi?"

AAP.

There are four victims and I only really know about the first and the second, and only a little at that. I wonder if Ooqi knows any more.

"What do we know about the body in Chinatown?"

MALE. NAME: HUANG FEN. MINER. FORTY-THREE. FAMILY IN CHINA.

"Any record of any kind?"

GAMBLING. REGULAR CLIENT AT MINING PLEASURE HOUSE.

That's right; the Chinese workers rotating through Nuuk and the mine include administration and logistical staff, miners and entertainment specialists – also called whores. The only Greenlanders employed at the mine are cleaners and one translator.

"But no criminal activity?"

NONE.

"What does Tan Yazhu say?"

THE BODY HAS BEEN PROCESSED, READY FOR RETURN TO CHINA.

"But no motive for the killing?"

POSSIBLE GAMBLING DEBT. HE IS INVESTIGATING.

"He doesn't think it is related to our investigation?"

HE HAS NOT SAID SO.

David's jacket slips from my shoulders as I reach for the coffee pot. I fill my mug halfway, pausing as another message from Ooqi appears on the screen.

DANIELSEN IS CHECKING IF CHINESE BODY IS MISSING PARTS.

"Okay."

ATII IS MEETING WITH CONTRACTOR.

"Good. What about you?"

There is a pause and I put the coffee pot down on the desk.

DO YOU REALLY WANT TO KNOW?

This is one of those moments when I realise that the quiet ones on the team are often the most dangerous, or the ones most likely to create problems, if not handled correctly. I should shut down the link, or visit the station, but Ooqi short-circuits my procrastination with a new window of text. It reads like a passage of Latin before the letters rearrange into something that could be very old English, before settling into Danish.

LOTS OF ACTIVITY FROM JONKHEER'S OFFICE COMPUTER. I AM MONITORING. SAY "OK" IF I SHOULD PROCEED.

"Okay," I say, before I can talk myself out of it.

The window dissolves into the screen and Ooqi's activity icon flashes to inform me he is AFK. I press the hint button on the screen and discover that it means he is *away from keyboard*. I just don't think it is likely and imagine him pulling out a second keyboard or working on another terminal or whatever he uses when he doesn't want to be traced. I decide that, given the circumstances, it is important to gather as much information as fast as possible. Whatever lead Ooqi is following, I trust him to be discreet. In the meantime, I could use a break.

I can feel a familiar sadness settling on my shoulders and I need to get out of the apartment. I call Iiluuna and smile as Quaa answers her mother's mobile.

"What are you doing today?" I ask.

"We're going to the Christmas Market."

It sounds like a good idea, and I arrange to meet them there as soon as Iiluuna joins the call. The sky is brightening, and I think I can see the sun as I finish the call and start to dress. Danielsen has provided me with a security detail and I think it is time to use him. I lock my apartment and take the stairs to the parking area. I wave to the police officer as I approach the patrol car, pausing at the passenger door as I notice a car parked with the engine running just a few cars away. The two men inside watch me as I climb into the passenger seat of the patrol car. They pull out of the parking space and follow us as we drive down the hill.

The officer assigned to me today is a young woman, and I am pleased that I remember her name.

"Natuk," I say, as she slows for the roundabout, "are we being followed?"

She looks in the rear-view mirror as she accelerates onto the road leading into town. She says nothing for a few moments, and then nods, just once.

"I think so," she says. "Do you want me to stop and find out?"

Even in the new Nuuk, with its expanded road system and new housing areas and communities, there is still very little road compared to towns and cities of a similar size in the rest of the world. To follow someone discreetly on vacant streets is an art form. The men in the car behind us are not artists, and when Natuk slows to a stop, snow crunching beneath the SUVs tyres, the men behind us stop too. The dilemma then is what to do next.

"I'll call for back-up," Natuk says, and reaches for her radio.

"No," I say. "Take me to the market. We have extra patrols there, today. I don't want us to pull any unit away from their assigned duties."

"But Danielsen said…"

"Yes, Natuk, I'm sure he told you to respectfully ignore my commands if my personal safety was at risk. But I am with you, inside a fast car, and they haven't broken the law yet. Let's keep going and see what happens."

"I'm not sure."

"Then call it in and tell the station where we are going."

I say nothing more until Natuk has talked with the duty officer back at the station, and we have pulled out into the road. The car behind us follows; matching our speed and parking close by when we enter the parking area of the old sports hall. I tell Natuk to relax as we leave the car and walk past the first market stalls inside. I smile as I remember that this was one of David's favourite places in Nuuk. The craft stalls with grotesque figures – *Tupilaq* carved from whalebone, and knives with ivory handles, brought the hunting culture of Greenland to the capital, as did the narwhal curry and sealskin furs. It wasn't quite the same, he would say, but we spent hours each Christmas at the market, haggling about prices with hunters and artists, sampling everything there was to eat, and quietly doing the rounds of the different stalls as David and I remembered the north, and our time in the settlement of Inussuk.

I let Natuk keep an eye on the men following us as I look for Iiluuna and Quaa. I feel safe around so many people, and I smile at the police officers in each corner of the sports hall. And then I feel Quaa's warm hand tickle my own, and she pulls me over to a stall to find her mother.

"This is Natuk," I say when I see the frown on Iiluuna's brow. "She is spending the day with me."

I smile again as Iiluuna wonders why Natuk is with me and then I feel a hand grip me by the arm. Stronger than Quaa's, I realise it is Natuk and she pulls me through the crowds, away from Iiluuna and towards the police officers close to the entrance.

"Reports are coming in of Calendar Man sightings in the city. We have to go," she says with a nod to the men following us. "The police in the market will stop them, and we'll go back to your apartment."

"That's not what I want to do," I say, but it is no good. I can feel Natuk's urgency through her fingers gripping my arm. I look around and try to catch Iiluuna's eye to say sorry, or Quaa's to reassure her that everything is alright, but Natuk pulls me into the cold Nuuk air, and a few seconds later we are in the car.

"They're going to stop them," she says, as she accelerates onto the road back to Qinngorput and my apartment. "Nikolaj will meet us at your apartment."

"Nikolaj? Didn't he have the night shift?"

"He's working overtime," she says. "We all are."

"Because of me?"

"Because of The Calendar Man."

It is confirmed then. Once my own officers start to use the media's name for the killer, he or *she* has become a legend, and the curse of Christmas.

Natuk turns up the volume of her radio as reports of suspicious activity at the market, and at other locations in the centre of Nuuk compete for space on the airwaves. It appears that a manhunt is underway as Natuk speeds me back to my apartment.

"This is ridiculous, Natuk. I am the Commissioner."

"Yes, ma'am."

She says nothing more until I am inside my apartment.

"Please lock the door, ma'am. Nikolaj will be here soon."

I am prisoner in my own apartment, while The Calendar Man has the run of the city.

Sapaat

Sunday, 7th December 2042

Chapter 7

I don't know how much of it is my fault, but I am starting to feel mollycoddled. Danielsen has effectively locked me in my apartment until my compassionate leave is officially over. Meanwhile, my police officers are racing back and forth across the city chasing a killer. They've been at it all night, and, according to the reports I can hear on Nikolaj's radio, they have found nothing. They might as well be chasing a ghost.

It's going to be okay, Piitalaat.

"No, David, it's not. If I'm stuck here I can't do anything. Can I? And you know how that feels."

"Ma'am?" Nikolaj asks, as he taps my bedroom door with his knuckle. "Are you alright?"

"I thought you were asleep on the couch?"

"I heard voices."

"It's just me, arguing with a ghost."

"Ma'am?"

"Don't worry about it. I'll get up and make breakfast soon."

"Okay," he says, and I hear him drift back to the lounge, together with the frustrated radio chatter.

I wait a moment to hear if David has more to say and then pick up my phone and log in to the police server. There are no new updates, and the task force activity icons show that Danielsen and Atii have, finally, gone home. There's no sign or record of Ooqi's activity, but I know he is there.

"Ooqi?"

A new window loads onto the screen, together with the false text. This time it is a passage from the bible that rearranges itself into a text from a popular novel before Ooqi's message appears and I lower my voice to a whisper.

"Anything new?"

AAP.

"Okay. Tell me."

LOTS OF EMAILS FROM THE JONKHEER TO THE DANISH OMBUDSMAN.

"Anna Riis?"

AAP. JONKHEER IS CONCERNED ABOUT REFERENDUM. WANTS ASSURANCES.

"What kind?"

WANTS TO KNOW IF CURRENT ECONOMICAL AGREEMENT WILL BE SAME UNDER GREENLANDIC RULE.

I think back to the meeting in my office and recall that the First Minister struggled to look the Jonkheer in the eye. I remember Pipaluk Uutaaq receiving lots of praise for her negotiations, and that the Dutch rental payments for the land outside Nuuk would be a significant contribution to the Greenlandic economy. In a curious twist of fate, Greenland's most valuable resource is not the minerals buried beneath the land but the land itself. Of course, no-one knows the details of the negotiation, nor the actual sum to be paid by the Dutch.

SOME CONCERN ABOUT RELATIONS, TOO.

"Explain."

CULTURAL DIFFERENCES. RACISM. WHAT HAPPENS IF DANES LEAVE.

It must be difficult for the Dutch. The Greenland colony is just an experiment, a toehold for the people of Holland, as their own country is threatened by the rising water levels that no dike can withstand. The world is warming, and the sea ice is melting, but it doesn't change the fact that Greenland is located at a much higher latitude than the Dutch are used to. The warmer climate has brought more snow, and the hours of light have not changed. It is just as dark as it ever was each winter, just as light in the summer. And then there is the language and the spontaneous nature of the Greenlanders that befuddled the Danes long before it confused the Dutch. I smile at the thought, as a new message from Ooqi flashes onto the screen.

NO MENTION OF CALENDAR MAN OR FRANKENSTEIN BODY.

Now that is curious, and I try to picture the Jonkheer, in his trim suit, and his warm hands, slightly chapped. He was concerned when we met, and the whole purpose of the meeting was, as I understood it, to request additional security at the *Sinterklaas* celebration. Perhaps it would be useful if Ooqi could look at the Dutch constabulary's communications.

THEY HAVE ARRANGED TO MEET TONIGHT.

"Okay," I say. "What about other mails and correspondence?"

YOU WANT ME TO LOOK AT THE CONSTABULARY?

"Haven't you already?"

There is a long pause and I wonder if Ooqi is hacking into the constabulary's server as I speak, and, if he hadn't before, did I just order him to do it? I'd like to blame it on Danielsen, to say that I was forced to seek alternative sources of information when my own police department kept me out of the loop. But I realise they haven't, there is just very little to report.

Besides, whether Ooqi had already hacked into their server, or if it he was doing it for the first time, both were just as illegal, and whether I ordered it or not was immaterial. Maybe I wouldn't have to retire after all? Perhaps matters would be taken out of my hands and I would be dismissed, as soon as Ooqi and I were exposed.

"I trust you, Ooqi," I whispered.

AH, MAYBE YOU SHOULDN'T.

It occurs to me that I have yet to hear his voice, and that, online at least, the shy police technician is quietly confident.

VICTIM: BENJAMIN DE KLOET. FIFTY-THREE. NO RECORD. MISSING FOLLOWING LIMBS: LEFT LEG AND FOOT. RIGHT FOOT. RIGHT FOREARM. LEFT HAND. CONSTABULARY INVESTIGATION ONGOING. SEARCH FOR MISSING LIMBS ONGOING.

"And the other body parts? Stitched to the body found in the Dutch administration building?"

CHARRED RIGHT FOOT. CHARRED LEFT HAND. TAKEN FROM BURNED BODY AT MORGUE.

"From Kong Frederik's Hospital."

AAP.

The window on the screen flickers with another cycling of fresh text before Ooqi returns.

SHALL I KEEP DIGGING?

"Yes," I say, and log out of the server.

I might still be grieving and locked up, but I intend to get back into the game. After all, the First Minister made a personal request for me to take responsibility for the investigation. By midnight tonight I will be officially back on duty, and despite his best intentions, Danielsen or my deputy police commissioner, won't be able to do anything about it. But I need to be prepared, and I need more information.

Nikolaj averts his eyes as I pad out of my bedroom in my pyjamas, but I have no time for his subordinate sensibilities, we have work to do.

"What were Danielsen's latest instructions?" I ask.

"Regarding you, ma'am?"

"Yes."

"I was to remain here and accompany you to work tomorrow morning."

"And I'm not allowed to leave my apartment?"

"Not without sufficient back-up," he says.

"Even shopping?"

"Not without back-up."

"Okay," I say, as I walk to the window.

The roof of the apartment block opposite steams in the midday sun, and the ravens spread their wings in the warm air. It is still chilly on the street, and I can see breath condensing on the windscreen of the car parked to the right of Nikolaj's patrol car. It is difficult to see the men's faces, but there are two of them, like before, but whereas the last two were of equal height, one of these men is significantly shorter than the other.

"Back-up you say?"

"Yes, ma'am."

I grab my phone from the bedroom and walk to the kitchen window, dialling as I stare at the car. I watch as the taller of the two men pulls a mobile out of his pocket and presses it to his ear.

"Brunch in ten minutes," I say. "And bring your friend."

I wave and end the call, smiling at the sigh I caught on the other end of the line as Gaba Alatak answered the call.

"Ma'am?" Nikolaj asks, as he hovers in the kitchen.

"Eggs in the fridge. Bacon and baguettes in the freezer," I say. "I'm going for a shower."

The pressure in the shower is good. Another reason we didn't move. The water drums on my body and I almost don't hear him.

Piitalaat.

"Yes, David?"

Having fun?

"I'm about to."

Be careful.

"You know I will." I smile as a thought occurs to me. "Past, Present or Future?"

What?

"Which ghost are you? Christmas Past, Present or…"

Just David.

We leave it at that and I turn off the shower as Nikolaj answers the door. When I step outside Gaba is making coffee as Nikolaj finishes the eggs. There is a bemused Greenlander in the hall, and I brush past him to change in my room. He is still there when I come out again, but this time he is holding a bacon and egg baguette in one hand, and a mug of coffee in the other. I smile and walk into the kitchen.

"What about yesterday?" I ask Gaba as he pours me a coffee. "Were they your men?"

"*Aap.*"

"You couldn't have told me?"

"I thought about it."

"You pushed my security detail into overdrive," I say. "Nikolaj was pulled in to do an extra shift."

"And my men spent the night outside your apartment," Gaba says, as he sits down; the chair creaks beneath his muscled frame. But he looks tired and I wonder when he started the morning shift.

"If I'd known," I say.

"You would have called and told me to send the men home."

"Yes."

"I'm not going to do that, Petra."

"But this isn't about me; it's about Nuuk, or the referendum. You're wasting resources."

"The men are getting paid."

"And you?"

Gaba gives me the look that he often wore as a police Sergeant, the one that doesn't invite any further comment.

"Fine," I say. "But I'm going nuts here. I've even started talking to David."

Gaba's look softens beneath his frown, the one that threatens to wrinkle his bald head.

"Stop that," I say. "It's just a calming device I'm sure. Nothing to get worried about."

"If you say so."

"I do, and once you're all finished with brunch, we're going out."

"Danielsen said…"

"Nikolaj," I say, as he protests. I point at Gaba. "Let me introduce you to Greenland's former head of the Special Response Unit, Gaba Alatak. If he isn't back-up, I don't know what is."

"But he's not on the force."

"No, he's not."

"And not armed."

"Nikolaj," Gaba says.

"Yes?"

"Constable?"

"That's right."

"This is your first time in Greenland?"

"Yes."

"Then you have a lot to learn. We might have tightened up on gun control over the past few years, but you can still buy a pump-action shotgun over the counter at the supermarket. Without a hunting licence. Don't make the mistake of thinking we're not armed. In Greenland, in the city, the towns and the settlements, you're never more than a few metres from a gun. Remember that."

"Alright, stop scaring him, Gaba," I say. "We're going out."

"Where?"

"The morgue, the supermarket, and then Little Amsterdam."

"The supermarket?"

"Yes, we're going to need supplies for the stake-out."

It feels good to be doing something. To be talking charge again. Catching the doctor off guard at the morgue was a bonus. I let him talk us through the bodies, pre-mutilation, while Gaba's man waits outside the door. There is something familiar about the face of the young man, and it has nothing to do with the tattoos on his fingers. I take a long breath and feel Gaba's reassuring grip on my arm. I lean against his body as I breathe out.

"And the age of the burned body?" I ask. "Any ideas?"

"I'm not a forensic dentist," the doctor says, "but I can say that it was a woman, in her twenties. The number of cavities in her teeth is typical for Greenlanders living outside of the city, and those who can't afford private dental care. She was short for her age. She was not a child."

"Have you seen the Chinese body?"

"Haven't seen it. Haven't been asked," he says. "I'm not surprised. It's rare that they involve us in any medical emergencies."

"But it does happen?"

"Not yet."

"And the Dutch?"

"What about them?"

"Do they ask for help?"

"Yes, if they need it. Part of the climate colony deal was providing health care," he says. "We have some regular Dutch patients, and we visit the outpatient clinic in Little Amsterdam."

"And do they contact you in the event of a death?"

"There hasn't been one yet, but I imagine they would. Why?" The doctor flicks his gaze from me to Gaba. "Am I missing something?"

"Thank you for your time, doctor," I say.

Gaba walks beside me on our way out of the hospital with his man in front of us and Nikolaj three steps behind.

"What now?" Gaba asks.

"We get supplies for our stake-out."

"You're enjoying this?"

"I'm enjoying being active, Gaba. It stops me feeling sad."

Apart from discussing what to buy in the store, I say little until we find a spot to park two cars in Little Amsterdam and we settle in for a cold night with a good view of the Dutch administration building.

"Why here, Petra?" Gaba asks when he calls my mobile.

"It's a hunch," I say. "I want to see who goes in after hours, and if they come out again."

"And this is related to The Calendar Man?"

"Quiet, Gaba. Someone's going inside."

Ataasinngorneq

Monday, 8th December 2042

Chapter 8

I'm still stiff from sleeping in the car through the night when I walk to the screen in the room set aside for the task force, but it feels good to be *doing something*, and I smile as I bid everyone good morning. I linger for a second or so before starting as I catch Ooqi's eye. He has yet to say a word, but I feel as though I know him best, at least where this investigation is concerned.

"Yesterday was the second day of advent," I say, "and, as far as we know, it passed without incident."

Atii nods and Danielsen shifts on his chair in search of a more comfortable position. They both look tired, and Aron's arrival with the coffee is well-timed.

"Aqqa is still in charge," I say, with a nod to Danielsen, "but I wanted to just go through a few things before we begin, just to catch us all up, and to let you know of a potential development in the investigation."

I pause to slip the digital thimbles over my thumb and index finger, and then I start casting images and the relevant notes onto the wall screen behind me.

"Victim one, unidentified, has some links to my past, but until we discover who he is, I think we need to shift our focus." I glance at Danielsen and wait for his reluctant nod. "Victim two, female, in her twenties, also unidentified. I think discovering their identity is key, and we need to focus – stop chasing ghosts, and jumping at shadows. The suspect – whoever he or she may be – has us running all over Nuuk, reacting to the next sensational act or murder. We have to stop that. We have to start anticipating what might be next, and where, and we need to be smart about how we do that. Any ideas?"

"About identifying the bodies – the first victim at least," Atii says. "I appreciate you don't want us to focus on you, but have you explored the link? Do you have any ideas how you might do that?"

"One," I say, and I am surprised I haven't thought about it before. "I'll look into it as soon as we are done. What about the young woman? Do we have a missing persons report that we might have missed?"

Many years ago, that was my job, handling the missing persons cases, the most sensational being the Tinka Winther case when the daughter of the then First Minister went missing, and Maratse found her body. It feels like such a long time ago.

"That sounds like a job for Ooqi," Danielsen says, as he turns in his chair to look at the younger police officer.

"No, I have a job for Ooqi," I say. "Perhaps you can follow up on that, Aqqa?"

"Alright," he says, but I can see he is not wholly convinced.

"Unless you have another lead?"

"I was going to check in with the Dutch constabulary."

"No need," I say. "The victim was Benjamin De Kloet. I plan on meeting the Jonkheer either today or tomorrow. I'll follow up on that."

"Missing persons then," says Danielsen.

I almost smile. It's the same with a lot of the police officers who come from the settlements. The idea of spending a day inside with the computer feels like torture. David was the same, although Sergeant

Aqqa Danielsen is far more computer proficient than David ever was.

"Thank you," I say. "Is there anything else? Atii?"

Atii stands up and joins me at the front of the room. She double-clicks her own thimbles and takes command of the wall screen. A few clicks and casts later and the screen is filled with a temporary profile in bullet form. She talks us through it.

"The Commissioner is correct, we don't know the sex of the suspect, or even if there is more than one, but if we assume there is only one, then we believe they are physically strong due to the lifting and positioning of the bodies, and they are most definitely smart – they either have knowledge or are able to act on knowledge that they have access to. For example, I have to go back to the IT contractors today to interview one of the employees who was sick. Based solely on the morgue robbery, the suspect either had knowledge of the camera systems upgrading or they knew they would be offline and planned accordingly. The suspect is also quick to react to local events, such as the screening of Frankenstein. If you've read the media coverage of the robbery at the morgue, and the *monster* discovered in Little Amsterdam, you'll agree that the suspect knows how to inspire the media to achieve his or her goals."

"What about motive?" I ask.

"I think the alphabet theory was a good one and discovering the first three letters of your name – plus the tattoos on the first dead body – it made sense, ma'am."

"And now?"

"It seems that the best motive might be the referendum after all. That the suspect is intent on creating a level of fear among residents in Nuuk, enough to keep them indoors and stop them from voting."

"And yet there were plenty of people at the market on Saturday," I say.

"Because we had plenty of police available. Visible, and tired," she says. "I think the suspect has been quiet these past few days to wear us down, have us chase our own tails, so he or she can plan the next move. A few prank calls were all it took over the weekend to stretch all the patrols to the limit."

"And you think something is coming?"

"*Aap.*"

"I agree," I say. "So, let's get out there and chase our leads, feed the information into the server, and meet back here first thing tomorrow morning, unless something breaks, of course."

I shake my head as Ooqi stands up and ask him to wait with a discreet wave of my hand, not discreet enough to escape Danielsen's eye. He frowns for a second before he strolls out of the room. I shut the door when he and Atii have left.

"I saw the Ombudsman go into the Dutch administration building late last night," I say to Ooqi. He presses his glasses further up his nose, and I smile at the fact he could easily have his eyesight adjusted, and then I realise the glasses are more than just a physical aid, they function as his covert computer terminal. He nods for me to continue, and I see a stream of date reflecting from the lens of his glasses onto the surface of his eyes. "Can you confirm it?"

"*Aap.*"

His voice is soft, almost inaudible.

"And can you see if there has been any activity,

any record of what they discussed."

"Not possible," he says.

"What would you need to do to find out?"

Ooqi reaches into his pocket and pulls out a tiny disc. He places it on the desk between us.

"I need to get that close to the Jonkheer's computer. Within a metre. He has some new firewalls I can't get around."

"And this," I say, as I pick up the disc, "will give you access?"

"*Aap*," he says. "Maybe you can do it?"

I thought he might say something like that. Regardless of the ethics surrounding bugging the Dutch administrator's office, or, rather, bugging it even more, I can't see another way of exposing what could be a motive to disrupt the Greenlandic vote for independence. If the Jonkheer truly was worried about the future of the Dutch climate colony and the survival of his satellite community, then the question was just how far would he go?

"I'm not sure," I say.

"It will help with the investigation."

"I know. I want to see the Jonkheer anyway. Perhaps he will give me the information willingly."

"Maybe."

"I'll think about it," I say, as I slip the disc into my pocket.

I give Ooqi's shoulder a squeeze as I walk towards the door. It could have been collegial, or even motherly, and I decide it is a squeeze of concern, and I follow it up with a question.

"Are you sleeping, Ooqi?"

"*Aap*," he says. "A little."

"Make sure it is enough," I say.

We all need to sleep more, I think, as I see yawns stifled behind folders and hands as police officers pass me in the corridor. Even Aron looks tired as I enter my office.

"The First Minister wanted you to see this," he says, as he scurries from his desk with a folder in his hand. "She has found sufficient funds to put private security guards on all public buildings."

"Gaba will be pleased," I say, as I read the note. "Starting immediately, I can see."

"Yes, ma'am."

"Good." I give Aron the folder. "Do you drive, Aron?"

"Yes, ma'am."

"Right then. Get a car from the pool and meet me at the entrance in five minutes. We're going to pay the Jonkheer a visit."

Aron pales and I wonder if he knows what Ooqi wants me to do in the Jonkheer's office. But his innocent face and gentle nature are the perfect foil. *Besides,* I think, *the Jonkheer brought his assistant to a meeting, why can't I take mine?*

The thought niggles as Aron drives to Little Amsterdam, and then I feel a little rush of something that feels like adrenalin, more than I am used to of late. I can also feel David's voice ready to issue his warning, but as much as I love him, and miss him, I can't take him with me inside the administrator's building. I need to be clear-headed, and I need to leave my ghosts in the patrol car.

It has to be done, and it has to be done now. I get out of the car and zip my jacket up to my neck, trapping a few strands of my long black hair in the plastic teeth of the zipper. It takes forever to tease them free, and by then we are inside the building and I am roasting in the Dutch heat. It seems that they have yet to find a happy medium between freezing and fiery temperatures. The Jonkheer's secretary is in short sleeves, and the sight of her pale arms brings a little colour to Aron's cheeks. *Finally*, I think, but I keep the thought to myself. As for my own cheeks, I am sure the word guilty is spelled across both of them, but I regain a moment's composure when the secretary brings us tea and small *stroopwafels*, David's favourite.

"He'll see you now," she says when we have finished our tea.

"Thank you for the tea," I say.

"Did you like it?"

"It's unusual, but pleasant."

"It's Rooibos," she says, as she presses two envelopes of tea into my hands. "Good for the heart and against colds and influenza."

"Thank you," I say.

I slip the tea into my pocket and follow the Jonkheer's secretary to a thick panelled door. The office is empty as we walk in and the secretary shows us to the chairs in front of the Jonkheer's desk. She leaves us, and I almost place Ooqi's disc beneath the stand for the Jonkheer's computer screen, but I am distracted by a large photograph on the wall of the Jonkheer and two children. They have his eyes, the girl especially.

"That's Esmée on the right," the Jonkheer says as he enters the room. "She's the oldest. And that's her brother, Hugo. A little scamp. Three years younger than his sister. Esmée is fourteen."

"Are they in Holland?" I ask.

"For the time being, yes. They are in one of the Vaalserberg towers, built on the highest point of Holland. I agreed with their grandparents that they should come once we have settled in."

"And your wife?"

"No," he says, as a sad smile flattens his lips. "She passed away some time ago." He gestures for me to sit down. "I understand you have also lost someone close to you. How are you doing?"

"Better each day," I say, and I wonder if that is true. "It helps to keep busy."

"Yes, I know," he says. He nods at Aron and then sits behind his desk. "Of course, we are very busy at the moment. You heard about the incident around *Sinterklaas*?"

"Yes, but we haven't been given any details."

"That's my fault. I was in shock. I wanted to handle it quietly, but I forget that this is such a small town in a small country. You can't hide something like that."

"No, you can't."

I slip my hand inside my pocket and pinch Ooqi's disc between my fingers. There is a space between the cushion of my chair and the wooden frame. We are sitting so close to the Jonkheer's desk that I can kick it. Well within one metre. I can easily press the disc into the gap if I lean forwards. But I pause as the door opens and the little rush of adrenaline peaks as the Ombudsman Anna Riis enters the Jonkheer's office; she has a stack of books in her arms.

"Commissioner," she says. "This is a surprise."

"Yes," I say. I stand to greet her and she drops one of the books on the floor.

"*Twelfth Night?*" I say. "That's Shakespeare."

"My favourite bard," she says, as she picks up the book. "I was going to lend it to the Jonkheer, but perhaps you would like to borrow it instead."

"Oh, I'm not a reader."

"You might find it useful."

"Useful?"

"Interesting. That's what I meant to say." She presses the book into my hands and walks around me to the Jonkheer's desk. "I've something a little heavier for you, Coenraad. Julius Caesar, as promised."

It's suddenly awkward, and I nod to Aron that we can leave.

"Petra," the Jonkheer says. "I'm pleased you came."

"Me too. I'm hoping we can start again," I say, "and that you will be ready to share what you know as soon as possible."

"Yes, yes," he says.

"Well, I just wanted to check-in and to see if you were alright."

"Thank you."

There is an awkward pause as the Jonkheer and the Ombudsman wait for Aron and me to leave.

"Your office is always welcome to contact us. You know Aron," I say, as he stands up. "He's my personal assistant, and you only have to call."

I'm rambling, and it's time to leave. I see the Jonkheer glance at my chair, and the adrenalin that I found so weak before, spikes to embarrassing levels.

"You dropped something," he says and walks around his desk. "Ah, Rooibos. Good for colds." The Jonkheer smiles as he hands me the tea. "I will be sure to have the constabulary contact you first thing tomorrow with an update on the body."

"Thank you," I say, as my heart recovers after another spike of excitement.

Aron is the first to reach the car and he opens the passenger door for me to get in.

"Back to the station?" he asks.

"No, take me home," I say. "I think it's best to quit while I'm ahead."

"Ma'am?"

"Don't worry about it, Aron. Just drive."

I'm sure Ooqi can find another way to listen in to the Jonkheer.

Marlunngorneq

Tuesday, 9th December 2042

Chapter 9

The brief lull in the Calendar Man's activity passes the moment Nikolaj knocks on my door and tells me he is taking me to meet Danielsen at Atuarfik Samuel Kleinschmidt, the school closest to the centre of old Nuuk town. It is also close to the parliament buildings and the refurbished police station. It's within short walking distance of everything, and now it's on the map of crime scenes chosen by the Calendar Man to strike fear into the people of Nuuk. I can see it has worked, too. The children huddle together with parents and teachers as we arrive and the head teacher declares the school is closed for the day. Head teachers have rarely needed an excuse to close a school for the day in Greenland, but in this case, I have to agree with him. I wait in the car until the children have dispersed and then Nikolaj takes me to the school entrance.

I recognise the advent calendar taped to the window at once, the fingers and toes in the snow beneath it are unfamiliar, although I have an idea where they might have come from.

"The toes came out of the twentieth window," Danielsen says. "The fingers were behind the fourth." He pauses as the head teacher hovers just behind us.

"I'll be in my office," the head teacher says. "At least for the next twenty minutes."

He stumbles over the ice in front of the door and I nod for Nikolaj to go with him.

"Go on," I say to Danielsen.

"I think we both know where the fingers and toes came from, but we'll check them for fingerprints, and get the doctor to match them with the body parts we recovered in Little Amsterdam."

"We have the body?"

"*Aap*. The Dutch Constabulary brought it to the morgue just before we got the call from the school." Danielsen's breath mists between us as he sighs. "The numbers," he says.

"Yes?"

"Four is the letter *A*. And twenty is *T*."

"Alright, Aqqa, what does that give us?"

"Including the number nine on the apartment door in Chinatown?"

"Yes, including that."

"Including that we get *PIITA*."

"That's Piita," I say. "Or *Peter*, if you spell it in Danish."

"It's also the first five letters in your name, ma'am."

"Oh, come on, Aqqa. This isn't about me," I say, and wave my arm at the advent calendar and the blood freezing to the window. "It's a coincidence."

"But the tattoos on your fingers…"

"A coincidence, Aqqa. And until we know who that man is, it will remain a coincidence. That's all."

I wonder if it's fair to let go at Aqqa like this. He's doing his job, and he's looking out for me, his boss, the Police Commissioner. I have to remind myself of the title, more and more with every new day in December. The department is overworked. Half of them are worried about me, and the other half thinks it is because of me.

"I should have retired, already," I say.

"What's that?"

"Nothing. You didn't hear that." I scuff at the snow beneath my boots, stamping it into a hard triangle before looking at Aqqa. "Alright," I say. "Let's move on. Next step."

"Identify the fingers and toes, as far as possible."

"Agreed."

"Find Piita."

"Definitely. Most definitely agreed. He could even be our first victim. Wouldn't that be a break, eh?"

"Yes, ma'am."

"Okay," I say, as Nikolaj walks out of the school building.

He turns and locks the door with a key from a large bundle at the end of a sealskin cord.

"The head teacher gave me the keys," he says. "What do I do with them now?"

"Leave them with me," Danielsen says. "And then take the Commissioner to the station."

"Not home?"

"No," I say. I'm almost tempted to stamp my foot. I look at Danielsen. "Call Atii and have her find Piita. You take care of the fingers and toes."

"Agreed."

I turn to head for the car but stop as soon as I see Danielsen reach for Nikolaj's arm.

"No," I say. "No more counter-orders. I'll dig into my past, these tattoos," I say, as I hold up my hands. "And we'll see you back at the station."

"Where are you going, ma'am?"

"Nuuk Media Group," I say. "You know the way, Nikolaj."

I'm quiet in the car, and the sound of the tyres rumbling across the compacted snow jars my thoughts into order. I'm not angry at Aqqa. I would never be angry at him. But this case is proving impossible. We need a break. Perhaps the killer has given us one? But then the question would be *why*?

I tell Nikolaj to wait in the car, or the canteen, but to give me some space. He might have heard stories about my past, but he doesn't need to know all the details. Few people do. Aqqa knows a little, Gaba a little more, but only two men know the full story. One of them cared for me and loved me until the day he died. The other is the director of Nuuk Media Group, and he clears his schedule a few seconds after I knock on his door.

"I need to know what you discovered twenty-four years ago. Anything that might be relevant to this case."

"You mean what I published?" Qitu asks.

"Let's start with what you didn't," I say, as I remove my jacket and flop down into one of Qitu's comfy chairs.

"I published almost all of my notes, edited of course. But one thing I never revealed had to do with Tertu."

"Tertu?"

The name is familiar, and I remember something about her being on television, an interview, together with Qitu. She even met with the Minister for Education, Culture, Church and Foreign Affairs – Malik Uutaaq, Pipaluk's father. It was his big break and a significant comeback from the scandal surrounding his involvement in the disappearance of Tinka Winther. The other details are sketchy, and I have blocked out even more than that.

"Tertu was my source on the story about the man who gave you those tattoos," Qitu says. "She even lived with me for a while. She and her baby."

"She was pregnant? Who was the father?"

Qitu says nothing, and, as much as I don't like to imagine it, I know it before he says the name.

"The man who gave you those," he says.

I rest my hands in my lap and stare at my palms. Qitu presses his hand on my shoulder as he walks to the other side of his office to make coffee. A sadist gave me these tattoos, and years' worth of counselling, nightmares, and anxiety. It was David that pulled me through, and I can feel the sadness welling up in me as I am forced to revisit the events surrounding my abduction.

I'm here, Piitalaat.

"No, David," I whisper. "Not anymore. You can't help me anymore. I have to do this alone."

I press my lips together and close my hands into fists as Qitu places a mug of coffee on the table in front of me. He is quiet. He watches and waits. Ready to speak and I nod for him to continue.

"Tertu decided to keep the baby. She said it was worth it, as if one good thing could erase so much pain. That's what she said."

I understand, more than I think Qitu could know, perhaps even more than David did.

"You were with her when she gave birth?"

"*Aap.*"

"And she stayed with you?"

"Until the boy was about ten months old. And then she just disappeared. I went to work one day, and the spare keys to my apartment were in the door when I came home. She was gone."

"A boy?"

"*Aap.*"

"What was his name?"

"I never found out. She didn't name him while he was an infant."

I look at my hands again.

"Did Tertu have tattoos? Did *he* give them to her?"

"She had tattoos before him," Qitu says, as reaches out to take my hand. "Her fingers were covered like yours, except her thumbs. She managed to run away before he did them."

"That's good," I say, as I gently tug my hand out of Qitu's.

Qitu waits as I drink my coffee. It's quiet in his office, such a contrast to the bustle I can see between the desks through the thick glass of the office window. A wild thought occurs to me and I glance again at the thick rectangles inked into the joints between my fingers. It's just possible that they were done out of love. I don't mean by *him*, the very thought creases my lips, stirring Qitu into a concerned fidget.

"What would Tertu tell her son, do you think? About his father?"

"I can't begin to imagine," Qitu says.

"But if she wanted her son to grow up thinking he was loved, do you think she would tell him everything, or just the good things – if there were any – about his father?" I put my mug on the coffee table and study my hands. Qitu moves his head for a better view of my lips. He reaches out to brush my hair to one side, and I lift my head. "Sorry," I say. I often forget he is deaf.

"What are you thinking?" he asks.

"I think her son might have tattooed his own fingers," I say. "Out of love, for his mother. Do you think that's possible?"

"It's possible. Of course."

"The problem with this case – The Calendar Man – is that my officers, the ones closest to me, keep trying to link everything to me. I just need to prove it's not about me."

"Why?"

"Because if I don't, then we will never solve the case. We will be looking in the wrong direction. It's all misdirection," I say, as I stand up, quickly. *Too* quickly. Qitu steadies me as blood and bad memories rush to my head.

"Petra?"

"Yes?"

"Sit down."

I let him lower me into the chair, and I smooth my palms on my thighs, backwards and forwards. I stop when I feel myself rocking. I can almost see David by my side, uncertain as to what to do as I rocked back and forth with the pain of rehabilitation.

"I think he would have done it," I say. "I think her son would have tattooed his fingers just like his mother's, if he loved her enough."

"I'm sure he did."

"It would have been a while ago, when he was young and impressionable. Perhaps he was hurting?" I say. "What happened to Tertu? You never said."

"I never saw her again, but I did get a call from a hospital in Denmark. She had named me as next of kin. When they found her body, they called me."

"She's dead?"

"An overdose. They never said anything about her son. It's a few years ago now. He would have been about fifteen."

"Then he would have been in the system. Maybe in a Children's Home in Denmark."

"Or in Greenland," Qitu says. "I'm sorry; I don't have any more information."

It was enough, I thought, and convenient if the killer was attempting to deceive us with misdirection. If he found Tertu's son, and if he was the first victim. A lot of *ifs*.

I almost miss Atii's call as my thoughts reel inside my head. I feel the vibration of my mobile humming through my jacket pocket and into the chair. I swipe my thumb across the screen as soon as I have the phone in my hands.

"Atii?"

"*Aap*," she says.

"You've found something?"

"Danielsen told me to dig through the missing persons files looking for a man named Piita."

"Yes?"

"I found two, in Nuuk, and I've talked with both of them today."

"You've talked to them?"

"*Aap*. One was missing earlier in the year; he was on a hunting trip near Kangerlussuaq. The other one was missing for three days. Drunk, at his girlfriend's house. She was drunk too."

"Any deaths? I mean dead *Piita*s?"

"*Naamik*, but Ooqi ran a quick search of the Children's Homes in Greenland."

"Yes?"

"A thirteen-year-old boy called Piita was admitted to the Children's Home in Maniitsoq in 2032. His record shows he self-harmed, something about his fingers. He pricked them with a fishing hook."

"Piita? You found him, Atii," I say. "That's our first victim. I'm off the hook."

Pingasunngorneq

Wednesday, 10th December 2042

Chapter 10

I sit at the back of the room as the Calendar Man task force work through the latest developments. Atii has a lead on Piita and wants to visit Maniitsoq, a small town north of Nuuk. It's an hour or so by plane – still the most effective and cost-efficient way to get around Greenland, and I think she should go. Danielsen is not so sure, and I wait as they discuss the pros and cons of sending one of the task force out of the city. I have decided to be nicer to Aqqa and give him more control of the daily running of the task force. Of course, it could be that I'm just relieved that the links between me and the murderer are becoming increasingly tenuous. My phone shivers with a message and I realise I never did explain to Iiluuna what happened at the Christmas Market, and why I had to leave so suddenly. I accept her invitation to dinner tonight, and then sip my coffee as Danielsen relents, and Atii makes travel arrangements.

"She'll be gone two days, weather permitting," Danielsen says aloud. I nod, and he continues. "I want to do a wider search for information. Go door to door at each crime scene, starting with the school – we'll work backwards."

Now that Gaba's security guards have taken some of the weight off the department, Aqqa has more officers at his disposal. Going from house to house will also make us more visible, and hopefully calm the people of Nuuk as well as giving us more information to sift through. I glance at Ooqi as he casts a map onto the wall screen and Aqqa circles the locations with a beam from the thimbles. Each area is marked, working backwards from the school, the Dutch administration building, the apartment in Chinatown, the empty lot by the housing block, and the steps outside the community centre opposite the supermarket. Five locations, four bodies, and assorted bits.

"What about the morgue?" I say. "That's also a crime scene."

"*Aap*," Danielsen says. "But the doctor has already told us as much as he can about the robbery."

"But maybe he has more information about the bodies." I put my cup on the tray at the back of the room and stand up. "I'll go and see him."

"Do you have time, ma'am?" Danielsen asks.

He's right to ask, of course he is, and I know that Aron is thinking the same thing – the daily stack of administration tasks is piling up. It was substantial before David died, and despite Aron's best efforts, the daily reports, intelligence, budget approvals and requisition orders have accumulated, especially with the Deputy Commissioner away on a course. But I have discovered that if I am active – no matter how disturbing the case – then I can get through the day without thinking too much about David. This is all part of the recovery process, I tell myself. I still need time. I need to ease myself back into the job. If I can do something useful at the same time, contribute to the investigation rather than slip into another bout of grief as I pore through reports at my desk, then the admin can wait. Besides, the First Minister wanted me personally involved.

"I have the time," I say. "But I want to talk to Ooqi before I leave."

Danielsen's frown is deeper this time, but he shrugs it off with a question.

"You'll take Nikolaj?"

"Yes, Aqqa, I will take Nikolaj."

He is satisfied, and the meeting is over. Ooqi follows me to my office. He waits by the door as Aron presses a few papers and a digital pad under my nose. I sign and give my thumbprint on three of the more urgent items and ask Aron to leave the rest on my desk. Ooqi closes the office door as Aron bustles into the outer office.

"I failed, Ooqi. You know that."

"Yes, ma'am."

The corners of Ooqi's mouth begin to crease and I realise he has found another way past the firewalls.

"You're in, aren't you?"

"*Aap.*"

I knew it, of course, but I sigh for effect, playing the role of the exasperated Commissioner.

"And?"

"Not much. An email to his mother asking about the children."

"Nothing to the ombudsman? No reply from Anna Riis?"

"Not yet."

I'm disappointed, and I slump into my chair. I'm taking a chance with this line of inquiry. It is both daunting and exhilarating, but less so when nothing happens, when there is nothing to report. However, if there was, I would have to decide just how to share it with the group. I look at Ooqi. Maybe he has an idea about that, a way of casually slipping the information into the collective pool of data.

"Danielsen is suspicious," he says. "He thinks you are withholding information."

"I am, sort of."

"He blames me."

"Ah," I say. "Is that a problem, Ooqi?"

"Not yet."

"Alright. Well, so long as you do your other tasks…" The thought makes me pause. "What other tasks are you doing?"

Ooqi's cheeks colour as he shifts from one foot to the other.

"Ooqi? *Constable*?"

"The Chinese are a little more alert than the Dutch," he says.

"What does that mean?"

"They discovered someone snooping inside their system and they have taken steps." Ooqi shrugs. "I'm locked out."

"And Danielsen?"

"Heard me curse at my desk the other day, and he guessed what I was doing."

"What did he say?"

"Nothing. Yet."

Ooqi gestures at the door and I nod that he can go. I watch as he stops by Aron's desk, just for a second, but enough to suggest that the two shiest officers in the Nuuk Police Department have something in common. They might even be friends. I realise how little I am aware of the social relations between my officers, and I decide that I must do more, that I must get back in the game, as it were.

Piitalaat.

I've been in the office too long. I text Nikolaj and arrange to meet outside the station. I don't know how much he has slept since the beginning of December. We make a good pair.

Nikolaj parks outside Kong Frederik's Hospital

and I follow him to the morgue. The walls are panelled with wood, pine, like the thick façade and beams of the outside of the building. Danish architects have won awards for their Greenlandic buildings. The designs incorporate a lot of wood – which Greenland doesn't have – and huge glass windows to let in the precious light at the cost of large surface areas susceptible to heat loss. Greenlandic buildings then, are a constant paradox of aesthetic design, politics and pride, often at the sake of practicality. I don't mind, the building is pleasing to the eye, and the pleasant interior has a calming effect. But I'm pleased I don't see the hospital's budgets, and I shudder to think of the running costs. Nothing is cheap in the Arctic. Something the Chinese and the Dutch are learning daily.

One of Gaba's security men stands outside the morgue, and a technician – perhaps one of the Nuuk contractors – fiddles with a wide-angled camera above the door. He steps to one side as we walk in. I glimpse the patch on the security guard's shoulder and think once again of Âmo and the spirit's long protective arms curling in from both sides. I wonder just how far they reach.

"Petra," the doctor says, as we approach his desk. "I was going to call you."

"Oh?"

"Yes. I found something of interest." He pauses. "I admit, I didn't think to check – what with the robbery and all the media. I have been a bit distracted. I apologise."

"What have you found, doctor?"

"The age of the burned victim."

"Yes."

"She's three weeks old. Three and a half, to be precise."

"Three and a half weeks?"

"Give or take a day or two. Actually, we can pinpoint the day, if I am correct."

I don't mind the doctor using my first name, but I don't care for his riddles. But, for the sake of cooperation and positive relations between our organisations, I try to smooth the crease I can feel on my brow.

"The victim was not burned at the scene," he says.

"We found a can of fuel and burn marks," I say.

"Yes. That's right. I'm sorry, the victim was *burned* at the scene, but that's not where she died." He pushes back his chair and stands up, turning screen on his desk towards us. "I won't bore you with the science of carbon dating, but I can say there has been significant progress in allowing for and eliminating radiocarbon levels in the environment, to use forensic carbon dating to determine the age of a body, and, in this case, the degradation of the skin." He walks over to one of the freezer doors in the wall and opens it, pulling the corpse of the charred woman into the room with a soft rumble of oiled wheels. "The skin was already burned before it was burned at the crime scene."

I lean over the corpse as the doctor points at the area where the arm was removed prior to being stolen.

"It was after the robbery that I could see a difference in the tissue." He grins, clearly pleased with himself. "The killer's first mistake," he says.

Killer. I'm beginning to wonder.

"When I started to look more closely, and after applying rudimentary carbon dating methods, I sent a sample to the university – the archaeology department. I even invited some geologist friends from the natural resources office to have a look."

"And?"

"We all agree. The victim died in a fire three and a half weeks ago. She did not die at the crime scene."

"You're certain?"

"Yes."

"And the cause of death?"

"Smoke inhalation followed by trauma associated with the flames. She burned to death."

I step back as I try to think where I was three and a half weeks ago. It was before David's funeral. We had just decided that he should rest, and give up the fight, no matter the cost. I couldn't go on seeing him in such pain, and when I realised he was fighting for me – always for me, never for himself – I told him to let go, so that we both could.

"Ma'am?" Nikolaj says with a soft touch of my arm.

"Yes?"

"Are you alright?"

I'm not, but we need to move on.

"When did you arrive in Nuuk?"

"Late October," he says.

"And do you remember a fire, in Nuuk?"

"I know when it was," the doctor says. "That's how I can be so precise."

He beckons for us to follow him to his computer and clicks on a headline from *Oqaasaq*. The fire occurred inside an older workshop used to paint vehicles. The sprinklers were clogged with paint, the article says, and the base coats and the clearcoats burned with surprising intensity.

Who was surprised, I wonder. I glance at the woman's corpse and realise she would have been overcome very quickly.

"No casualties," the doctor says. "According to the article."

"So, her body was removed."

"Yes."

"During the fire?" I say. I tap the screen and highlight the word *intensity.* "If she was an employee, she would be missed."

"The fire occurred at night."

"Then she was there out of hours."

"Maybe she broke in," Nikolaj says. "Together with the killer."

"Killer," I say. "In this instance, he is an opportunist, until we can prove otherwise." I look at my watch. I have somewhere I need to be. "Let's get this information to Danielsen and Ooqi. We'll add the workshop to the list of scenes to investigate, and interview anyone connected to it. Thank you, Bendt," I say, and he seems pleased at the familiarity. He's earned it.

Nikolaj drops me off at Iiluuna's apartment. He is reluctant to leave, and I'm forced to order him to drive home and rest. He waits until Iiluuna answers the door and seems satisfied when she hugs me and draws me into the cosy interior that smells of cinnamon and candle smoke. Nikolaj drives away as Iiluuna closes and locks the door.

Quaa's hug is tight enough to bring tears to my eyes, and I clutch her to my stomach as she stands on tiptoe to reach around my neck. Her fingers slip, and I lift her, just enough so she can clasp her fingers and complete the hug. Kicking off my boots and walking into the kitchen is a challenge, but neither of us want to let go.

"Quaa has something to tell you," Iiluuna says, as she sets the table.

"Really?" I press my lips against Quaa's head and whisper. "What is it? Are you going to get a puppy?"

"*Naamik*," Quaa says, and giggles.

"A new pair of ice skates?"

She shakes her head.

"Then I don't know," I say, as she lets go and slips out of my grasp. I feel a slight tug of sadness as she runs to her room, but then she returns, just as quickly, carrying something behind her back.

"Put it on," Iiluuna says.

Quaa lifts a green wreath onto her head, fiddles with a button at the back, and then beams as four digital candles flicker and twist between the pine needles. Quaa's brown eyes twinkle in the light and I struggle not to cry, again.

"You're going to be Lucia," I say.

"*Aap*."

"Sankta Lucia," Iiluuna says. "And not just at her school. She is going to be Sankta Lucia in *Katuaq*, at the Christmas concert. The First Minister is going to be there."

"Saturday," I say, as Quaa sits at the table.

Iiluuna dims the lights and we eat roast seal and rice with a thick brown sauce. David would love it, and I hope he'll forgive me, but when Iiluuna suggests it, I agree to spend the night.

Sisamanngorneq

Thursday, 11th December 2042

Chapter 11

Iiluuna's apartment is near the centre of Nuuk, and within walking distance of the police station. I can still smell the sweet cinnamon rolls and see the candlelight flickering in Quaa's earthy brown eyes as I dip my chin inside the high neck of my jacket and brush wayward strands of my black hair beneath my wool hat. Breakfast was a delight, and I was actually hungry, sipping my coffee and eating toast as Quaa sat on my lap at the kitchen table. We parted half an hour later as Iiluuna walked Quaa to school and I went the other way towards the station. With no new bodies, Nuuk Media Group had little to worry the city with other than the latest speculative polls and concerns that the supermarket is running out of sugar. The same happened last year when the Greenlanders competed with the Danes and the Dutch for Christmas ingredients. Vanilla was in short supply too, but not cinnamon. It seems we will never run out of cinnamon. Although, as I round the corner and check for traffic before crossing over to *Aantuukasiip Aqqutaa*, it looks like someone has spilled a bag of cinnamon in the snow.

Except it isn't cinnamon, it's blood, and there is more than a bagful.

I follow the trail of blood-drenched snow all the way to the body of an elderly woman, Greenlandic, maybe seventy years old. Her arms are stretched straight above her head, hands tied. Her legs point at ninety degrees from her waist. A closer inspection shows the ankles are bound too. I call the station on my phone and try to corral the stream of pedestrians to the opposite side of the path. I try to keep them moving. I fail.

It's not far to the station, I can almost hear the cough of one of the old Toyota's as the engine starts and it drifts out of the car park and around the block. The patrol car's blue lights reflect across the pale faces of the onlookers as they squint into a new swathe of snow that dusts the body on the ground and obscures the camera lenses of their mobiles. I'm less worried about the mobiles, and more about the advent calendar that I spot tucked beneath the victim's head. Whoever left her here was worried about the wind blowing the calendar away. I wait until the evidence team has photographed and bagged the calendar before looking at it. The window for December twenty-second is open.

"I'll put it with the others," the crime scene investigator says.

"They're in the evidence room?"

"Yes."

"I can see them?"

"We've got them laid out on a table along the far wall. You can't miss them."

"Thanks."

I see Natuk talking with the pedestrians. All of them arrived at the scene after I did, but I let her work the line. Perhaps someone knows the victim. There is no mortuary ambulance service in Nuuk, not currently, and I walk beside the paramedics as they are reduced to porters, their life-saving skills are not needed. It's a shame, I think, as I study the victim's face. The soft lines of her cheeks are filled with a dusting of snow. She must not have seen her attacker, or he was too fast for her to react.

I'm making assumptions again. When did the

attacker become a *he*? Is that Qitu's fault when NMG dubbed the killer *The Calendar Man*? And is *he* really a killer, or simply an opportunist with an agenda?

Without thinking, I reach out and squeeze the old woman's hand, just before the paramedics load her into the back of the ambulance. Atii is following up on the first victim, Piita, while Danielsen directs officers to explore the crime scenes. I found this little old lady, and I decide that she will be my responsibility, as I push thoughts of paperwork to one side, again, and choose to work on my rehabilitation. I find it hard to believe that no-one knows this latest victim. I'll contact the local artist we bring in for sketches and have her work with the photos from the crime scene. Qitu has a new headline, but I want this lady's face on the front page. I intend to find out her name before the end of the day.

I wait until the paramedics have gone, and then I walk towards the station, tugging Natuk gently by the arm as I walk past her.

"I want you to work with our artist," I say. "And have Qitu put her picture in the paper. He can stream it as soon as we send him the file."

Natuk nods and makes a new note in her notebook. Digital pads and tablets don't always work in the cold, and a pencil and pad of paper are required tools even in 2042. Some things don't change.

"I'll be in the evidence room," I say, as Natuk tucks her notepad inside her jacket pocket. "Meet me there when you are finished with the artist."

"Yes, ma'am."

We part company just inside the door, and, when I'm finished banging the snow from my boots and dusting it from my shoulders, I take the elevator down to the basement, and sign-in to the evidence room with a thumb scan. The lights flicker out of hibernation into a working intensity, and I see the calendars laid out as the officer had described on a long table at the end of the room. The light catches small pools of wet snow on the floor. The evidence team have already been here.

The long walls to my left and right are concertina cupboards on rails that open with a winding handle, or the press of a button. I ignore them and concentrate on the calendars.

There are five advent calendars including the latest one I found this morning. The numbers are sixteen, nine, twenty, one and twenty-two. If I add the number nine from the Chinatown apartment between the second and the third calendar, I get the following letters:

P I I T A V

There is a roll of wrapping paper and a thick marker at the end of the table. This must be the table they use to prepare evidence that needs to be transported. I tear off a square of paper for each calendar and write the letter associated with the number on each one, adding an extra *I* as agreed with the task force between calendars two and three. I finish as Natuk enters the evidence room with a folder under her arm.

"That was quick," I say, as she shows me the artist's sketch of the victim.

"It's a preliminary drawing before she feeds it into the computer. I thought you'd like to see it."

"Thanks." I nod at the folder. "What else have you got?"

"A few images from the scene. The body and the calendar." Natuk hands me the folder and walks up and down the row of calendars. "Why have you put a letter *I* between these calendars?"

I forget that she has not seen all the evidence and explain about the supposed link between the apartment door in Chinatown and the Calendar Man.

"And you're using the alphabet."

"It's Atii's theory," I say.

Natuk takes the folder from my hand and shuffles the photos at the end of the table. She shows me the image of the woman and traces the letter *L* with her finger.

"The shape of her body," she says. "Do you see it?"

"Yes."

"So," Natuk says, as she writes the letter on a new square of paper. "It goes at the end." She steps back and reads the letters aloud. "P I I T A V L."

"It used to spell *Piita*," I say.

"Hmm," Natuk says, as she looks at the photo again. She swaps the *L* and the *V*.

"Why did you do that?"

"The calendar is under the woman's head," she says. "The killer wanted us to see the body first."

"I thought it was because of the wind."

"Maybe. But the wind was light this morning. It hasn't really blown for a few days."

She's right. But switching the last two letters doesn't give the word anymore sense.

"P I I T A L V," I say. "It's just as meaningless as before."

I watch as Natuk studies the photograph; almost smile at the way the tip of her tongue peeps through her lips as she works. It reminds me of Quaa and the icing sugar. But I stop smiling as Natuk slowly turns the letter V upside down.

"It's an A," she says with a triumphant smile. "Look. The calendar was upside down." She points at the woman's head in the photo and taps the calendar. "Santa's feet are pointing up the way. He wanted us to turn the letter around." Natuk grins and then places the photo on the pile at the end of the table.

I know I should praise her analytical skills, and even suggest that she looks at the other evidence we have on the task force wall, but I can't quite distract myself from the new arrangement of letters. The P and the two Is followed by the other four letters of my nine-letter name.

Piitalaat.

"Yes," I say, more to David than Natuk, but she seems pleased that I agree.

Natuk steps back to take a photograph with her mobile, but I stop her with a light touch on her arm.

"For the files," she says. "I can cast it to your wall."

"Not yet," I say.

"I don't understand."

"I know, but I want you to trust me. Let's see if Qitu has published the sketch yet. I just want to know her name, or if anyone is missing her. You can send the picture to Ooqi or Danielsen after that. Okay?"

"Yes, ma'am."

Natuk is a pretty young Greenlandic woman, and the puzzled lines around her mouth complement her. She is still wearing them as we leave the evidence room and enter the elevator. Aron is waiting in the hall as the doors open, and the sight of the papers under his arm and the tablet in his hands almost distracts me from the Natuk's interpretation of the latest piece of the Calendar Man's puzzle.

"Can it wait?" I ask Aron.

"This?" he says, with a quick glance at the folder. "Yes, this can, but there's a call for you. It's Qitu at NMG."

"In my office?"

"Yes," Aron says, as he shuffles alongside us as we walk along the corridor to my office. "He says he knows who the woman is. That she died last night in the retirement home."

"How does he know?"

"Qitu has an aunt in the next room. He was visiting her last night when the woman passed away. He saw her face as the staff prepared her body for the family to see her. They are flying in today. There is a chapel in the retirement home, and she was put there for the night."

"There are no guards at the retirement home?"

"No, ma'am. They're only in public places," Aron says. "Places open to the public," he adds. "The retirement home is only open to staff and relatives of the residents."

"Natuk," I say.

"I'll go straight there."

"Thank you."

I watch her leave and hope she remembers our deal. I want the victim's name before my own is dragged back into the investigation.

"Is everything alright, ma'am? Can I get you some coffee?"

"Hot water," I say. "For tea. Use the bags we got from the Dutch secretary."

I walk into my office and hang my jacket on the back of the chair. There is a light flashing on the telephone and I pick up the handset.

"Qitu?" I say. "It's Petra."

There is a delay, and I picture Qitu reading the transcript of my voice on the screen of his phone before he replies.

"I know the woman's name," he says. "She is Ivaana Qaavigaq. She was seventy-five."

"And you saw her last night?"

"I saw her after she passed. I have seen her a few times, each time I visited my aunt."

"Do you think her death was natural?"

"I can't say, Petra."

"But there was no sign of a struggle while you were with your aunt? The staff didn't say anything?"

"They said they had been expecting it. So, I suppose it was natural then."

"I suppose so."

I let the phone slip down my cheek as I think about the woman passing away peacefully in her own bed, only to have her body desecrated by a coward. An opportunistic coward. That's what I think of him now. He isn't worthy of the title *killer*. But he has to be stopped all the same. If there is a connection between him and I, if it isn't just misdirection, perhaps there is a way to expose him, and bring him out into the open.

"Petra?"

"The referendum," I say.

"*Aap*?"

"You have not mentioned much about it in the paper."

"The Calendar Man has taken up a lot of column

space, that's true."

"Save some space for me in the next edition," I say. "I promise you an exclusive."

"Petra," Qitu says and laughs. "That's sweet, but NMG has a monopoly on the news in Greenland these days – both the sensational and the investigative pieces."

"As a favour then," I say, as I put the phone down.

Tallimanngorneq

Friday, 12th December 2042

Chapter 12

Atii is due to report in and I wait as Ooqi sets up the wall screen. Aron brings in the breakfast rolls and a plate of *klejner* – they remind me of twisted donuts, but denser. Another seasonal cinnamon creation we have inherited from Denmark. Another fried pastry to plague Danielsen's waistline. He catches my eye as he takes one and I wonder if Natuk has told him anything. The softness in his eyes suggests that she has, which I should have expected, but that he cares, which I should accept. But what I can't accept is the so-called Calendar Man's methods which I find as cowardly as they are repugnant.

"Atii's ready," Ooqi says and we turn to face the screen.

The image of Atii's face moves as she jogs through the snowy streets of Maniitsoq. The sky is lighter already here in Nuuk, but it feels as though Atii is working in the night. There is a police officer slightly ahead of her, and the shadow jostling in and out of the camera's vision on her right suggests there are at least three of them.

"Atii?" Danielsen asks. "Are you there?"

"*Aap.*"

"And what are you doing?"

"Following a lead," she says. Her breath mists in clouds in front of the camera and the view bounces as she increases speed. Her words come in waves as she runs down the street. "We're going to pick up a captain of a fishing trawler."

"Why?"

"He had Piita's body on ice," she says. "For over a week."

"On the boat?" I ask.

"*Aap.*"

We can see the docks now, and the pancake ice bumping in the water. Another week of low temperatures and it might be strong enough to walk on, if it wasn't for the fishing trawlers doing their best to keep a channel open.

"Piita was working on a trawler," Atii says. "Some of the men, including Piita, got drunk, and there was a fight. One of the crew strangled Piita. The captain put Piita's body in the hold, with the fish, on ice."

"In Maniitsoq?"

"*Aap.* But the boat was in Nuuk at the end of November." Atii pauses at a signal from the police officer in front of her. They slow, and we see the Maniitsoq police officers draw their sidearms. Atii lowers her voice to a whisper. "We arrested the crewman in a bar last night. He confessed to killing Piita but knows nothing about what happened to the body. He hasn't talked to anyone. Now we want to pick up the captain. He sleeps on the boat."

"Atii," I say. "Was Piita's body on the fishing trawler when it came to Nuuk?"

"We think so. But the crewman – the one who killed Piita – was kicked off the boat. He's a cousin of the captain."

"And the captain was protecting his cousin."

"*Aap.*" Atii adjusts the camera angle so we can see her face. "The captain is known to be violent, and we believe he is armed. We're going in now."

Atii clips the camera to her vest. The sights of her pistol are just visible as her body stiffens at a quiet command from the Maniitsoq police sergeant. We can hear them breathing. Aron opens the door and steps into the room. Danielsen hushes him with a look.

"That's it," Atii whispers. "We're going in."

It's been a while since I was a part of a team tasked with picking up a suspect and I grip the edge of the desk in front of me. I hold my breath as Atii's camera shudders on her vest and we can hear boots slipping and stomping across the hard snow. She turns, and we see the hull of the trawler. We see the railing as she climbs over it and hear the soft thud as she lands on the deck.

I remind myself that Atii spent several years on the Special Response Unit when Gaba was her boss not her husband. She is a competent officer and an excellent shot, but she has two boys now, and I worry suddenly that she is in danger. So are the other officers, but I don't know them. And yet, I am equally responsible for them. I snap out of my thoughts as one of the police officers shouts a warning to the occupants of the trawler. We can see his hand on the door handle.

"Police," he shouts. "We're coming in."

Atii moves into position, her hand slips into view as she presses it onto the shoulders of the officer in front of her, just as he opens the door. My vision is fixed on the sights of Atii's pistol. It is as if the pistol is glued to her body and her head as she moves through the wheelhouse of the trawler to the stairs leading below decks. We hear something rattle and thump in the darkness as Atii follows the police officer into the trawler's kitchen. A sudden flash of orange and an explosive boom makes me jump, and then we hear three shots, we see three bursts of white, and then we follow Atii as she steps over the police officer on the deck in front of her, kicks a shotgun to one side, and presses her knee on the body of a man bleeding at her feet.

"Suspect secure," Atii says, and I am amazed that her voice is so calm.

I want to know about the police officer from Maniitsoq, the one who disappeared beneath the flash of the captain's shotgun.

"Status?" Atii says.

It takes three or four long seconds before we hear the officer's voice.

"I'm alright," he says.

Atii turns and we see the third officer help his Sergeant to his feet.

"Danielsen," Atii says.

"Go ahead."

"The captain is dead. I'm sorry." There is a crackle of static as Atii removes the camera from her vest and looks into the lens. "I'm going to have to stay another day or two to write this up."

"Understood."

"Atii," I say.

"Ma'am."

"Good work."

"Not so good, I think. I had some questions I hoped the captain could answer."

"I understand, but you're unhurt. That's good. And you have confirmed Piita was dead before he was dumped outside the community centre. That's important information. We can use that to move the case forwards."

"How, ma'am?"

"We're going to draw him out," I say. "Write up

your report and get back to us as soon as possible."

Ooqi casts the case notes and images onto the wall screen as Atii closes her camera link. I study the notes for a second and then step up to the screen.

"Piita was dead before the perpetrator used his body. Based on Atii's report and her interview with the crewman, I think we can assume that Piita's body was taken from the fishing trawler when it was in Nuuk."

"The Calendar Man must have known it was onboard," Danielsen says. "He must have known the captain or someone on the crew." He pauses for a second. "It's not a very big trawler. The crew might have been just two or three men."

"Piita, the captain and his cousin," I say.

"And the captain won't be able to tell us anything," Danielsen says. "We need to check with the Nuuk harbour records, and see when the trawler was here, and who was onboard."

A window pops up on the wall screen as Ooqi opens a link to the Nuuk Harbour administration office.

"What do you mean when you say you want to draw him out, ma'am?" Danielsen asks.

"I'll come back to that," I say, as I swipe the image of the second victim into the centre of the screen. I drag the image of the elderly woman alongside it. "Both these victims were dead prior to being used by the perpetrator. Based on this evidence, I don't think we can refer to him as a killer. More an opportunist and a coward with an agenda." I can feel the curl of my lip and I'm a little shocked at how personal the case feels. It's getting harder and harder to remain objective.

Focus, Piitalaat.

"I am focused," I say.

"Ma'am?"

"What?"

"Your focus?" Danielsen says. "It's the three victims. What about the Chinese body or the one found in Little Amsterdam?"

"If I'm right, then I'm sure we'll find that they died prior to being used by the Calendar Man – if they are related. The Chinese victim's body is probably already in China by now, and the Dutch have been slow to report any details," I say. I glance at Ooqi and he shakes his head, just slightly, but enough to suggest that we will have to use the official channels to find out more.

"And if they were dead already?" Danielsen asks.

"Then we need to force his or even *her* agenda. We need to know what the motive is. We need to take the initiative. Qitu is saving us some column space in the next edition of *Oqaasaq* – online and print. The news has been dominated by the Calendar Man, with very little reporting on the referendum. We need to change that and see if that is the driving factor."

"Unless you are, ma'am."

It's not clear to see, but I guess that Natuk has talked to Danielsen, or that he has been down to the evidence room and seen the calendars. I smile at the thought of Nikolaj bursting through the door at any minute, dragging me to a safe room at a nod from Danielsen.

"If I am," I say, as I walk away from the wall screen and sit down on the nearest chair, "then I think we need to use that. I want to make a statement. I want to be the one quoted in the media."

"What do you intend to say?"

I realise that I haven't thought that far ahead, but I remember Iiluuna saying that the First Minister was going to be at the Sankta Lucia Christmas celebration, and it occurs to me that I should talk with Pipaluk. She wanted me to take personal responsibility for the case. Perhaps it is time to show a united front, standing side by side on the stage tomorrow. I make a rule of leaving the majority of the press conferences to the media officer, or the investigator in charge of the case, but for once I think it is time to mix policing with politics, and to reassure the people of Nuuk with a more personal presence.

"It's risky, ma'am," Danielsen says.

"I'm willing to take that risk. You can double my protection if you feel it is necessary."

"Actually," he says, "I was thinking of the risk to the general public. What if you force his hand? What if he actually kills someone as a result?"

"Aqqa," I say. "We have doubled our patrols, to the limit of what the department can bear. The First Minister has contracted Gaba's security company, and he has guards all over the city – even the retirement homes, since yesterday. We have the city all but locked down. With the cooperation of the Chinese and the Dutch, we're making it increasingly difficult for anyone to do anything without being seen or stopped. It's time to up the ante and make a move."

"I'm not sure, ma'am."

"You don't have to be. I take full responsibility."

Aron shuffles to my left and I turn to look at him.

"I can set up a meeting with the First Minister," he says.

"Good," I say. "Invite Qitu to the same meeting."

Aron slips out of the room and the door sighs to a close. It is the last sound we hear for over a minute, although I'm sure I can hear Danielsen thinking.

"It's dangerous," he says.

"And necessary."

He sits down and taps his fingers on his thighs.

"I talked to Natuk. She showed me the calendars, and the letters beneath them. I think her interpretation is right," he says, and nods for Ooqi to cast the image onto the screen. "It's your name, ma'am. It has to be."

"But why?" I say. "If this is about me and my past, surely the only link was Piita – the son of the man who gave me these." I lift my hands to reveal the bands across my fingers. "Revenge died with Piita."

"Maybe it's not about revenge," Danielsen says.

"What then?"

"I don't know," he says, but I can see a shadow of an idea in his eyes.

"Aqqa? Say it."

There is another pause followed by the sigh of the door as Aron leans into the room to confirm that the meeting is set for tomorrow morning. Danielsen looks at Aron and waits for him to leave.

"If it's not revenge," he says, as the door closes, "it could be infatuation."

"That's ridiculous," I say.

"Maybe, but I think we need to dig deeper into your past, or maybe something more recent," he says, with another glance at the door.

Arfininngorneq

Saturday, 13th December 2042

Sankta Lucia

Chapter 13

The first time I met Pipaluk Uutaaq was in a mountain graveyard above the remote settlement of Inussuk overlooking Uummannaq fjord. She stood between her mother and brother as her father, Malik Uutaaq, took a non-partisan decision to join with the then First Minister as she buried her daughter on the mountainside. It was a unifying moment for the two political parties, during a period when Greenlandic culture and identity had more to do with the language one spoke than the country one was born in. I remember being moved by the First Minister's speech, when she repeated it in Danish. I remember holding David's hand as I felt what I believed to be the beginning of a new era of acceptance and opportunity for the people of Greenland. It was Malik Uutaaq who forged a new, more sustainable approach to Greenlandic independence, but following his death it would be his daughter who made it happen.

If, I think, *the people come out and vote.*

Pipaluk is thirty-seven now, and, if I admit it, slightly intimidating. She has an eye for fashion, projecting power and confidence through the colour and cut of her clothes. She captures her identity in the creamy curl of her narwhal earrings, and hints at her agenda in the shade of her lipstick and the delicate highlights on her cheeks and around her eyes. For my part I left David's jacket at home and smooth the crisp lines of my uniform with my hands as we sit at the distressed pine conference table in the room beside Pipaluk's office. Qitu wears the wrinkles and scents of another late night at the office, and he slumps in the chair opposite me.

Aron hovers at the end of the room beside Pipaluk's assistant. I smile at him as I scan the artwork on the walls, rough, like the conference table. There is a driftwood feeling in the room that has more to do with a fishing trawler than a government office, and it offsets the smoothly tucked hems of Pipaluk's sealskin trousers and black blouse. Like her clothes, the room signals identity. She is grounded, at one with the sea and the land, and my thoughts are drifting, bobbing from one image and association to another, a tide of memories as I try to avoid a niggling thought that bubbles to the surface each time I look at Aron.

Infatuation.

But that's not what this meeting is about, and I clear my mind as Pipaluk speaks.

"The doors open at four. The choir will sing two carols and then the children will walk in bearing candles – digital wicks, of course. Once the children are arranged in front of the stage…" Pipaluk pauses as she wipes the screen on the next page. "Then I will make my speech. Petra," she says.

"Yes."

"The speech is in two parts. Once I am finished with the festive address, I thought I would invite you to stand beside when I talk about the importance of the vote and the safety measures the city has put in place."

"Of course."

"Good."

Pipaluk's smile softens her professional demeanour, and I wonder if she has practiced it. It is strong enough to rouse Qitu into a more upright position.

Piitalaat. Focus.

He's right. I need to think, although thinking is what kept me up half the night.

"First Minister," I say.

"Yes, Petra."

"I'd like to add something to the speech. It's the reason I arranged this meeting."

"The speech is locked, *Commissioner*."

"It's just a comment I'd like to add, in connection with assurances we are making regarding safety."

I wait for her to respond, trying not to place too much weight on her use of my title, not my name, or the tiny wrinkles on her top lip as she straightens her smile.

"Go on," she says.

"It's nothing much, more of a continuation of the piece Qitu is streaming just after lunchtime today." I wait for Qitu to nod. "We've decided that each time we talk about the so-called Calendar Man, we use the words *coward* and *cowardly*. Together with the article we're working on changing the image of fear to pity and disgust, and we'd like you to do the same, First Minister."

"*We*," she says, and points a manicured finger at Qitu and me.

"The department, and *me*, specifically."

"You want the killer…"

"Coward," I say.

"You want him to think *you* are calling him a coward. Why?"

"Him or her, yes," I say.

I try not to glance at Aron, but I can feel him staring at me. It's difficult to determine how he is looking at me, as concern could so easily be mistaken for *infatuation*. Regardless of how I interpret my assistant's look, it is the First Minister's reaction that is more important.

"You're making yourself a target."

"Yes."

"I don't understand. Is it for the good of the people, to save the vote, or do you have information you're not sharing with me?"

"It's too early to tell," I say.

"So, you're testing a theory?" Pipaluk looks at Qitu, waits for him to focus on her lips. "You haven't said anything yet. What do you think?"

"I think," Qitu says, "that the Commissioner is making a mistake. Two mistakes." Qitu sighs as he looks at me. "I think you're underestimating the Calendar Man and underestimating the impact any link – tenuous as it may appear – may have upon you."

"I have to know," I say.

"But goading him puts you in danger. Danielsen agrees with me."

"Ah, you've talked to Aqqa," I say. I'm tempted to laugh, but instead I point at the shadow of Nikolaj just visible through the glass in the door. "Danielsen is the reason that poor officer isn't sleeping."

"You still haven't heard from the Chinese or the Dutch," Qitu says.

"No. I was hoping the First Minister could apply some pressure," I say.

"What do you need?" she asks.

"They have yet to confirm if the two bodies – one in each district – died of natural causes or if they were victims of the Calendar Man."

"What about the others?" Pipaluk leans forwards.

"Have I been kept in the dark? I thought we agreed that you report to me directly."

"I'm here, First Minister."

"Barely. Your mind seems to wander in between, and now Qitu says you have failed to take the situation seriously. Where is the Deputy Police Commissioner? Should he be here instead of you?"

Like the surf receding from the shore, I feel as though the purpose of the meeting is slipping through my fingers, and I am losing control, or I am about to.

"First Minister," I say.

I want to say more, but Aron cuts me off.

"I have sent daily briefings to your assistant, as per the Commissioner's request," he says, as he turns the tablet in his hands. Pipaluk's assistant confirms with a quick nod of her head.

"I see," Pipaluk says.

"While some aspects of the case have been unfolding, I have provided you with a full report, each day, following the Commissioner's instructions."

Aron glances at me, and I decide the earlier look in his eyes was in fact, and could only have been, concern. Nothing more. I would be foolish to think I have suppressed David's shadow. I am still grieving. Perhaps Pipaluk is right to infer I should be replaced.

"The Deputy Police Commissioner is in Denmark. He is on a course, after which he is taking leave, and will be in Denmark over the holidays. He will return just before New Year," I say. "However, if you feel that a replacement is necessary…"

"No." Pipaluk shakes her head. "I've been busy meeting with ministers. I confess I have followed the investigation in the media rather than your reports. I will be sure to take the time to study them once the

Sankta Lucia celebration is over. Perhaps we should get ready? I'll leave the wording of your part of the speech to your discretion," she says, as we stand. "But, Petra, please do listen to your colleagues." She glances at Nikolaj and Aron. "They seem to have your best interests at heart."

I whisper my thanks to Aron as we leave the conference room and Nikolaj leads us out of the parliament building. He stops as Qitu catches my arm, just before we cross the parking area to the police station entrance.

"You're sure about this?" he asks.

"Yes," I say. "The referendum is three days from now. We have to force his hand, give him a chance to make a mistake."

"And then?"

"Then we find the coward and stop him."

I have a good view of the centre aisle from where I stand in the shadows behind the podium. The choir is split in two sections, framing Quaa and the children walking with the halting step of Saint Lucy, their white gowns trailing on the floor, candles in their hands and a flickering crown on Quaa's head. It is a struggle, but I manage not to cry, and then I think of Iiluuna, and hope she is taking lots of pictures.

The children's voices sing the last refrain of Sankta Lucia and the audience settles in their seats, just as Pipaluk steps onto the stage. I have seen the Danish copy of her speech, and I follow her Greenlandic as best I can, using the speech as a guide. I know she will repeat it in Danish, but I want to be ready to step onto the stage on cue. I'll miss it if I am listening to what she says.

I feel a tug at my arm and turn to see Qitu. He leads me backstage and I nod at his friend Geert Aalders waiting by the door.

"Qitu, I'm on soon," I say.

"I know. I just wanted you to know that the article has been read over a thousand times since we posted at one o'clock. The comments are ticking in, and I have a team sifting through them. This one," he says, as he shows me his tablet, "is written in English."

"English?"

"A neutral language, perhaps. When you read the comment, you'll understand why."

I can just hear Pipaluk begin the Danish part of her speech, and then Geert interrupts us, as I take the tablet from Qitu."

"I'm going to find my seat," he says.

Qitu nods and I read the comment.

Caesar said: a coward dies a thousand times before his death. You, Commissioner, taste of death but once.

"We've traced the comment to a user account created for the purpose of leaving that one comment." Qitu takes my hand as I return the tablet. "It's a death threat, Petra."

"No," I say, as I force a smile. "It's Shakespeare." I glance over my shoulder. "I have to go, Qitu."

"Petra. Don't go out there. What if he's in the crowd? You've just made him mad enough to try and kill you."

"Mad enough to make a mistake, and then we'll catch him, Qitu. Thank you," I say, as I slip free of his hand and walk onto the stage.

The lights are brighter now. Less atmospheric, more political. I smile as Pipaluk steps to one side so that we can share the podium. I know what I am going to say, but I can see a copy of my part of the speech on the podium's screen. I plan to start by thanking the children and the choir, and then the First Minister, but the crashing of emergency doors and the sight of Gaba's security men ushering people out of their seats and into the lobby pushes the speech out of my thoughts. The First Minister's security team remove her next, as the audience begin to murmur, and the parents ignore the guards and grab their children from the stage. I look for Quaa, to see if she is with her mother, and then my view is blocked by Nikolaj's black jacket and all I can see is his body, as he presses me to his chest and drags me off the stage, through the backstage access and across the snow to one of the spacious SUVs humming in the snow outside the back entrance.

"What's going on?" I ask, as Nikolaj bundles me into the back of the SUV.

"Drive," he says, as he gets in beside me.

"Nikolaj?"

"Bomb threat," he says, as the officer behind the wheel weaves through the crowds fleeing the cultural centre. "Someone called it in as you were walking on stage."

"Stop the car," I say. "Turn around. We have to help these people."

"No, ma'am. I'm to get you home. Those are my orders."

Sapaat

Sunday, 14th December 2042

Chapter 14

They have been here all night and I can't remember how many times I heard them make coffee or knock softly on my door to hear if I was alright. I am being handled by Danielsen, riding high on some supposed authority the Deputy Commissioner has given him. Gaba isn't much better, as he plays the *old friend* card, together with his resources that he threatens to arm – within his rights – and turn Nuuk into a militarised state of martial law. They let me watch coverage of the fallout following the bomb threat at least. I still can't shake the images of people fleeing what should have started out as one of the more charming and festive Sankta Lucia celebrations I can remember. I excused myself after midnight and locked myself in my room to read the message from Iiluuna.

Her mobile needed charging, she wrote. She was sorry she couldn't message me earlier.

But you're safe? Both of you?

Aap.

That was all I needed. Confirmation that they are home. That the doors are locked. Quaa's big day has been spoiled, but it is a day she will never forget. No-one will. And it is all my fault at least that's what Danielsen insinuated, despite Gaba's more vehement conclusions that suggested the opposite.

When does Atii get back, I wonder, as I hear his raised voice once more. *Who is looking after his sons?*

They have turned my living room into ground zero, demanding regular updates from the station and fielding calls from the First Minister's office. At least I'm not alone. She is under lock-down too.

I'm frustrated and angry. I just don't know who

to direct it towards. Me or him? The Calendar Man. I think it is a *he* now, ever since reading the quote from Julius Caesar. It's such a masculine thing to quote. So dramatic. I'm tempted to look at it again, for the twelfth or thirteenth time tonight, but as I pick up my mobile, a new window flashes onto the screen. More encryption followed by the familiar ALL CAPS text.

COMMISSIONER?

"Ooqi?" I say, and picture the young officer typing in some dark corner of an even darker room.

AAP.

"What's going on? At the station?"

LOTS OF ACTIVITY. KIND OF FORGOTTEN ABOUT ME.

They have underestimated him again. The thought makes me smile.

"Anything new from the Dutch or the Chinese?"

STILL LOCKED OUT OF THE CHINESE SYSTEM. BUT HAVE ACCESSED DUTCH SERVER. MAN DIED OF HEART ATTACK. WAS BEING TREATED FOR HEART CONDITION.

"That's four out of five," I say.

AAP. IS THERE ANYTHING I CAN DO?

"Do you still have access to the Jonkheer's computer and mail?"

AAP.

"Anything of interest?"

NOT YET.

"And nothing more from the ombudsman, Anna Riis?"

NOTHING.

"Okay. Let me know the minute you get something."

I slip my phone between David's jacket and my pillow and lie down. My hair catches in the thick weave around the pockets of David's jacket, and I can smell him again, the smell of the north.

Piitalaat.

"Not now, David," I say. "I need to think."

It occurs to me that the Calendar Man is somehow plugged in to the life and, more importantly, the deaths in the city. He might be reluctant to kill his victims, but he is not squeamish about working with the dead. He has knowledge of butchery, which means he could be a hunter. I almost laugh at the thought of how unhelpful that it is – almost every man in Greenland is a hunter, and most women know how to butcher a seal. At least in the settlements. So, the Calendar Man might be from the north, or the east of Greenland. The population is greater on the west coast and in the south, with a higher percentage of non-hunters as generations of Greenlanders continue to adapt to city life and the service industry.

Focus.

"I will if you stop interrupting."

I bite my lip. I don't mean that. I wish he was here to interrupt. I wish he had never left. I want David by my side, not a pile of books weighing down the duvet. I want *him* hogging it, snoring, keeping me awake because he is here, not just because I miss him. And I do miss him. Terribly.

I feel the sudden need to visit his grave, and I peel David's jacket from my pillow. I slip my legs over the side of my bed and pause, pressing my toes against the floor; I can feel the rough fibres of my socks against my skin.

"None of the victims had been buried," I say.

The victims were either in the refrigerator at the morgue, in the cool chapel, or even on ice, as Piita was aboard the fishing trawler. The Chinese man's apartment was cold – he had stopped paying his bills, and the windows were open in the Dutch administration building.

"They weren't buried but they were all chilled, one way or another."

I don't know how important it is, but it's a fact, and I grab my phone and add a note to the file on the server. We can talk about it, if Danielsen ever lets me out of my room.

I return to my earlier thought and wonder how the Calendar Man is getting his information. He is scouring the city for dead bodies, so it makes sense if he has access to institutional records. But that doesn't explain how he knew Piita's body was in the hold of the trawler, or that the young woman burned to death in the fire at the workshop. We still don't know her name, but I have an idea that she knew Piita, or the Calendar Man. Perhaps both.

We need a new break in the investigation, and we're not going to get it stuck inside my apartment. I pull on David's jacket, stuff my mobile into the pocket and open my bedroom door. It's still dark outside, and the men in my living room look tired. None of us has slept, although Nikolaj looks like he might have tried from where he is slumped on my sofa.

"Petra?" Gaba says. "Are you alright?"

"Nothing happened, Gaba," I say, with a look at Danielsen. "Nothing."

"I had to take precautions, ma'am. We saw the

comment on the article, and then the bomb scare…"

"Misdirection," I say. "I'm still not convinced this is about me. But he's done it again – the Calendar Man. We're looking in the wrong direction, again. The First Minister has been saying it from the start – this has to be about the referendum. But we're not going to convince people of that from my living room."

"You can't leave your apartment, ma'am," Danielsen says.

"No?"

"You're a target."

"With the luxury of knowing where I go and when I go there, before he does." I frown as I look around the room. "Where's Aron?"

"I thought it best to leave him at the station," Danielsen says. He looks at his watch. "Of course, he'll be off duty now."

"He's my personal assistant, Aqqa."

"I know."

"And now he's a suspect?"

Danielsen glances at Nikolaj as he stands up. He gestures for him to sit down again with a wave of his hand.

"Under the circumstances…"

"You've made an assumption. I suppose you've taken him off the task force too?"

"I may have suggested he concentrate on clearing the paperwork on your desk."

"These are my decisions, Aqqa."

I never would have believed it before, but it seems clear now. There might be a reason Danielsen has been communicating so closely with the Deputy Police Commissioner. I would never call Danielsen a coward, but I recognise an opportunist when I see one.

"What has he offered you?" I ask.

"Who?"

"The Deputy Commissioner. Has he given you the nod for his position, when he takes mine?"

"Ma'am?"

"Is that what this is all about? This whole theory of yours about the calendar numbers being letters. Natuk had to turn one of the letters from a V to an A. It wouldn't have fit otherwise."

"Petra," Gaba says, as he takes a step towards me. He stops as I clench my fists at my sides.

"You've been shoe-horning this theory of yours into the investigation from day one, Aqqa. How do I know you're not trying to manipulate the investigation for your own personal gain, and the Deputy's?"

"That's not what I'm doing, ma'am," Danielsen says.

I don't hear him. Suddenly I'm reeling, and the kitchen is hotter than it was a second ago. Maybe it's David's jacket. He always wore it outside. It must be warm. I'm warm. I'm hot, and I'm starting to sway. I feel Gaba's hands on my shoulders as he guides me to a seat at the table. He presses a glass of cold water into my hand, smooths his palm over my brow and helps me out of David's jacket.

"I'll stay," he says to Danielsen. "You can leave an officer at the door, but the two of you should go home."

"You're not a sergeant anymore, Gaba," Danielsen says. "You can't tell me what to do."

"You don't think so?"

I reach out for Gaba's hand, squeeze it until he

stands down, and Danielsen slowly, quietly nods for Nikolaj to follow him out of my apartment. I wait until I hear the door close with a soft click, and then I let go of Gaba's hand.

"I'm alright, Gaba."

"No, you're not. I just don't know if it's because of Maratse or if this case, the links to you…"

"Can't it be both?"

I take another sip of water and then lower the glass to the table. The chill water condenses the glass, and my fingers are wet. I wipe them on the table and Gaba watches me.

"I don't know what the next move is," I say. "I feel as though I'm barely functioning as a police officer, and certainly not as Commissioner. I don't think I care if Danielsen has career ambitions. It might even be best for him to step up. He's making more decisions than me now anyway, and my assistant is covering the paperwork. Perhaps I should just step down."

"I don't think so, Petra. Not yet."

"Why? Because of this case?"

"It's high-profile. It needs someone at the top. Someone with a title. You can put Danielsen there, but he'll still only be a Sergeant. Even if the Deputy was back, he would only be a leader by default. You are the Commissioner, Petra, and Nuuk needs to see you. You need to be visible. If you were to slip away now, if Danielsen keeps you trapped inside your apartment, then this Calendar Man has won." Gaba reaches for my hand and it is his turn to squeeze. "You might not feel strong right now, but you can be strong again. I've seen you bounce back from much worse than this. I know you're hurting, and that you miss Maratse."

"I really, really do, Gaba."

"I know. But he would tell you the same if he was here, and he would do what had to be done if you were gone. He would hate it, but he would do it."

"This is your pep talk?"

"It's one of them," Gaba says and laughs. "Did I ever tell you why I changed the name of my company to Âmo?"

"You wanted to make it more Greenlandic?"

"It's a little more than that."

Gaba lets go of my hand and opens my fridge. He pulls out two bottles of beer and opens them. I don't remember buying them, but the beer tastes good and I smile as Gaba sits down.

"Âmo is the shaman's familiar spirit," he says. "You know when the shaman is inside the turf hut or the igloo, or whatever it was that our people lived in back then…" Gaba pauses for a swallow of beer. "Well, he's just got the whole crowd on the edge of their seats, the lights are low, it's warm, and his soul is just about to take flight, that's when Âmo comes in. He's got these long arms, and he wraps them around the people inside the hut, igloo…"

"Tent."

"Whatever. Anyway, he's got them there. It's Âmo that keeps them on the edge of their seats; he's protecting them while the shaman is off in the underworld, or some other magic place. Âmo makes sure the people are still there when the shaman gets back. They're trapped. Under his spell. And I like that. The idea that someone has got the shaman's back, while he is off solving problems, combing Sedna's hair for the sake of the hunters, or chasing down some mean old angry *tupilaq*. That's what I imagined. I mean, I loved being a police officer, but who looked after the police when they were off solving problems?"

"The police are the shaman in this story?"

"*Aap.*"

Gaba shrugs as he takes another swallow of beer.

"What are you trying to tell me, Gaba?"

"I'm trying to tell you not to worry. I'm trying to tell you to start doing your job. The people of Nuuk need you, and," he says and smiles, "I've got your back."

It's a stretch. I can't quite imagine the Commissioner as a shaman, but the thought that Gaba is looking out for me, an old, reliable friend in uncertain and unruly times, is enough to finish what I've started. The coward may have many deaths before he dies, but with Âmo by my side, I'm willing to taste death if it means I can get my life and my job back. On this second Advent of Christmas, it's time to stop hiding and start hunting.

Ataasinngorneq

Monday, 15th December 2042

Chapter 15

It takes a lot of convincing, but as soon as Gaba proves his kids are sleeping at his parents' house I let him sleep on the couch. Danielsen has a patrol car outside my apartment, anyway. But I can't sleep, and I pick up one of David's books and read the first few pages. It's clear that we had our own interests outside of work, and, after all these years, I can't see what he saw in science fiction stories. I admit, I don't read for pleasure, and I believe the smartphone was invented just for me. The new integrated models that they developed over the years are more intuitive, even more invasive, and so much more fun than David's books will ever be. I decide they are better as bed ballast, the physical weight of my thoughts, and a constant reminder. I close the book and place it on top of the pile on his side of the bed.

I liked it when he read to me, and I miss the rasp of his voice after he was finished with a chapter. That was when I was sick. It was therapy, and I remember those horrible moments when David realised he had forgotten to bring a glass of water to my bedside. His mouth would be dry, and I remember him fidgeting as he wondered if I would notice if he went to the kitchen and brought back something to drink. That's when, eyes closed, I would reach for him, and clasp his fingers between mine. I wouldn't let him go, and he would start another chapter, reading until his tongue stuck to the roof of his mouth, trapping the words behind his teeth. I didn't need the words so much as I needed to hear his voice, or just his breath. I needed to feel his weight on the mattress, and the rough scratch of his skin on my hands. It would take months before I actually listened to the stories.

That's all we have now – stories, the memories of what we did together. The things that happened to us, the decisions we made, and the way each story shaped our lives. David is gone, but I still have stories to tell. I'm saving them up for when I see him again.

I hear the sofa creak as Gaba crawls out of it. It's still dark, but I have survived yet another night without David. I dress for the day and when I smell fresh coffee I walk out of my room and join Gaba in the kitchen.

"Do you have a plan?" he asks, as he fills the toaster with thick slices of rough-hewn bread.

"To show my face. I thought about calling Pipaluk Uutaaq. I'll ask her if she'll join me on a walk along Nuuk's main streets."

"You're campaigning?"

"She can campaign all she wants. I just want to be seen, not hidden away. Will you walk with me?"

"Sure."

"I'll make the arrangements while you butter the toast. Bring some for the day shift too."

I press my phone to my ear to blot out the vigorous scraping of butter across thick toast. I laugh as I wait for my call to connect. There is little that Gaba doesn't do *vigorously*. I walk into the lounge and stare across the bay as I invite the First Minister to a walk through town.

"Security won't be a problem," I say, as Pipaluk hesitates.

I can hear her advisors in the background, but her sighs suggest she is just as frustrated as I am. We agree to start at the cultural centre, and then it's just a matter of convincing Danielsen's police officers that they still answer to me. Gaba's presence and reputation helps, and it's not long before we are parked beside the First Minister's car.

"I invited the Jonkheer," she says, as we greet each other in the parking area. "I hope you don't mind."

"I think it's a good idea," I say, despite the flush of adrenaline I feel as I think about Ooqi's illicit monitoring of his computer, the parts he has access to.

I recognise Geert Aalders as he gets out of the passenger side of the Dutch administration's saloon. He looks untidy when compared to the sleek form of the Jonkheer, Coenraad is taller than Gaba, but the slim fit of his winter jacket presents an almost willowy figure beside Gaba's robust form. Together with two Dutch Constables, a handful of Âmo security personnel, and my own close-protection team, the pedestrianised streets running through the centre of Nuuk feel suddenly narrow, and our entourage presses the shoppers and office workers to both sides of the street. We are more of a nuisance than a reassurance, and I split our group into three, with enough space between each group to allow pedestrians to slalom between us like a steam of fish through a coral reef. The First Minister's group is in front, and when she stops, we all stop.

"She's quite the showstopper," the Jonkheer says, as he walks towards me. "I thought we could talk for a moment while we wait."

"I'd like that," I say.

"But first," he says, "I have something for you." The Jonkheer takes a package from Geert and hands it to me. "*Stroopwafels*," he says, as I unwrap it. "I heard that you liked them."

"Yes," I say. "And a friend of mine – he was very fond of them."

"Ah, yes. My condolences. I heard about your friend. David, was it?"

"David Maratse. He was my partner."

"Partner? Not Married?"

I tuck the Jonkheer's gift inside my jacket pocket and start to walk as the First Minister's group moves along the street. The sky is light enough for the street lights to react, but still dark enough that the neon lights of the shops, offices, and apartments of Downtown Nuuk give a Tokyo-sheen to the snow-lined streets.

"We talked about it, but there were complications," I say. I can see Gaba a few paces behind us talking with the Jonkheer's assistant. "I was kidnapped in the beginning of our life together. David rescued me, but the following years were dark, and…" I stop myself as I wonder why I am saying this, but the Jonkheer wears a look that is a sympathetic as his clothes are sophisticated.

"Please, continue," he says. "If you want to." He gestures at the First Minister's group just ahead of us. "Pipaluk needs this, and the people need to see her. We have plenty of time."

"Alright," I say, as Pipaluk's group moves on and we meander behind them. "I suppose we had been through so much together that marriage felt too formal. It wasn't necessary, so long as we had each other."

The Jonkheer stops and reaches for my hand. "When you were kidnapped, is that when you got these… tattoos?"

"Yes," I say, and draw my hand back into my pocket.

"Forgive me," he says. "It's just I have been briefed by my senior constable. Your Sergeant…"

"Danielsen."

"Yes. He has been very forthcoming with information. And our own studies have concluded that there are many links between you and this Calendar Man. Do you agree?"

"There are some similarities," I say.

"More than a few, according to my men, and the evidence. We have been trying to establish the link between the Dutch victim and the others." He lifts his hands for a second. "I must apologise for our tardiness. Your department has shared information, whereas we have been silent."

"We did notice."

"And yet, you have exercised such professional restraint. I admire that. For our own part, I think we found the whole thing abhorrent to the degree that we were paralysed." He lowers his voice." You've seen the body?"

"Yes."

"Such horror. A real Frankenstein's monster. It was shocking. We were stunned, to tell you the truth."

"And now?"

"Now we have had time to collect our thoughts and process our data. My Senior Constable is meeting with your Sergeant today, but I wanted to tell you what we know, and what we have surmised."

I'm tempted to patch Ooqi into the conversation but decide to let Danielsen handle it. But I'm curious and almost impatient when the First Minister interrupts us.

"We're going to continue through town and on to the community centre," she says. "My assistant has called the media and they are setting up now. Will you join us?"

"Of course," I say. "We'll follow you."

The Jonkheer continues as soon as she is gone.

"Benjamin De Kloet died of natural causes. He had a heart condition, and was struggling to adapt to the cold, and a new lifestyle. I would never have put him on the list. He would have been better off and better suited to life in one of the Vaalserberg Towers, but he had some political sway, and climbed to the top third of an exclusive list."

"And he died of complications?"

"We believe he died as a result of his condition. It cost him his life."

"And he was treated by the colony doctor?"

"Yes. Benjamin called the doctor earlier in the day before he died. According to the doctor's records he arranged a visit and then cancelled it later. The post mortem of his body, carried out by the same doctor, determined that he was dead an hour or two prior to his body being mutilated." The Jonkheer stops as we near the entrance to the community centre. "The doctor has been quite disturbed by all this. He feels responsible, despite our best efforts to convince him otherwise."

I wait as the Jonkheer talks with his assistant. It strikes me again how the Calendar Man must have access to medical journals and information to find the bodies necessary to wage his terror campaign. The Jonkheer knew of Benjamin de Kloet's medical condition. What else does he know, and about whom? But even if he has access to the Dutch colonists' medical information, he can't possibly know about the Chinese or the Greenlanders. Not without some form of bugging device. I watch as Geert Aalders gives the Jonkheer something. Geert catches my eye as the Jonkheer walks back to me.

"Sorry, I was just talking with Geert about returning to the office." He points at the community centre. The light from the digital frieze casts stars across his dark blue eyes. "We won't be voting tomorrow. No matter what might have been agreed, and whatever we signed, we still consider ourselves guests in your country."

"It's your country too," I say.

"Yes," he says, and turns something small within his fingers. "And yet, we are still foreigners and I suppose it will take some time, perhaps even years, before we are able to trust one another. This doesn't help," he says and places a slim disc into the palm of my hand. "The cleaners found it last night," he says. "We don't know how long it has been there." He turns it in my palm. "If you look at the markings – very small, at the edges – they look like Chinese characters to me."

"Chinese?" I say, and I wonder if he can hear my heart thumping inside my chest.

"Yes." The Jonkheer lowers his voice. "I appreciate that we arrived after they did, but perhaps we can talk about this at another time. At your convenience, of course."

"Of course," I say, grateful for the splash of blue from the frieze above my head. It changes the hue of my cheeks from an embarrassed red to a healthy glow.

"Once again," he says, "please forgive us for our

tardiness. I promise it will never happen again, and if we uncover any further evidence that will help in your investigation, you will be the first to know."

"I look forward to that."

"Yes," he says, with a glance at the community centre. "You must catch this man, before he ruins what we have all worked so hard to achieve."

We shake hands and I watch him leave, pressing the disc into my pocket as the Jonkheer's assistant catches my eye for a second time, staring until the Jonkheer steps between us and the Dutch contingent walk back to their vehicle.

"Petra?" Gaba says. "What was all that about?"

"I think I just dodged a bullet," I say.

"Really?" He points at the retreating figure of the Jonkheer's assistant. "Not from where I was standing."

CHRISTOFFER PETERSEN

Marlunngorneq

Tuesday, 16th December 2042

Chapter 16

Aron shuffles a stack of folders in his arms at the rear of the assembly hall as the duty officer briefs the day shift. It is voting day, and all leave has been cancelled, bonuses promised, and favours cashed-in. I wait for him to finish with the practical details, and then join Danielsen at the podium. He starts with a profile of the Calendar Man.

"We're looking for a male, in good physical shape. We don't believe he is Chinese. We honestly don't know if he is Greenlandic or European. He's intelligent, and motivated. He's also an opportunist and experienced in low-cost disruption. We're not trying to anticipate what he might do. We believe that if we do our job right. Look in all the usual places, check the back entrances regularly, and basically use common sense policing, we will foil all but the most elaborate plan. As for a description, based on the nature of his activity, he is likely to be wearing practical clothes." Danielsen pauses at a shuffling of feet and a few suppressed laughs. "You're right; he'll look like everyone else on the street. But pay attention to his hands – if he's wearing gloves, they are more likely to be insulated work gloves than fleece. He'll be wearing a backpack, big enough to fit one of these," Danielsen says and holds up one of the advent calendars inside its plastic evidence bag. "The last calendar was left with the body of an elderly woman close to the shopping mall. The calendars have been left with bodies, or they have contained body parts – I'm referring to the advent calendar left at the school." Danielsen pointed to where Atii and Ooqi stand at the rear of the room. Atii will be in one of the SUVs reserved for reports concerning the Calendar Man. Ooqi will be coordinating everything via uplink, and we want you to feed relevant data directly to him. Contact Atii directly with sightings and critical incidents. Ooqi will be patched into her channel and will collate everything, pushing data to your patrol tablets with priority messages if there is an incident." Danielsen takes a step back from the podium, and then remembers something. "Oh, and I'll be with the Special Response Unit on standby here at the station."

"Thank you, Aqqa," I say, as I step up to the podium.

I can see fifty police officers in front of me, and the duty officer has confirmed that another thirty are already on the street, at the close of their shift. Twenty more police officers are at home, or relaxing, voting, shopping and enjoying their day off, but ready to respond, should it be necessary. I hope it won't be. We're already stretched thin and eating into the next year's budget. Or was it the following year? I don't remember. But it should be the last thing on my mind as I look at the men and women waiting for me to speak.

"There's been a lot of speculation," I say, "as to the Calendar Man's motives, and even his target. It has been suggested, several times, that it has something to do with me. And, several times, I have believed that to be the case. Some of you have felt that more than others, pulling extra shifts to provide protection – for me. Or responding to incidents at the very end of their shift – because of me. Well, now that we've established who's to blame…" I pause for a few laughs and many tired smiles. Too many. "It's only fair that I ask you to do one more thing. Not for me this time, but for your country. Today Greenland votes, one more time – perhaps the very last time – on its future. Today, what you do, *everything* you do, is for Greenland. To give the Greenlandic people the chance to vote, not just for their future, but yours, our children's future, for every child from this moment forwards. Now, if this sounds a little dramatic, then allow me to be selfish, and angry for just one moment, because this is not about me." I take a step towards Danielsen and pluck the advent calendar from his hands. "One cowardly opportunist, no matter his motive, is not going to stop the people of Greenland making a decision on their future. We're not going to let him. *You're* not going to let him."

The first sporadic claps echo around the assembly hall as I press the calendar into Danielsen's hands. I raise my own hand for them to stop clapping as I step up to the podium.

"One more thing," I say, as the men and women of the Nuuk Police Department clasp their hands behind their backs. "I'm not going to tell you how to vote today, but I am going to remind you to *remember* to vote. This is your day too. Now, go make it safe for everyone."

I catch a few words and comments as the officers disperse and get ready to hit the streets. It feels good to see them straighten tired shoulders, to clap each other on the back as they leave the assembly hall. I feel like a Commissioner again, for the first time in a long time, certainly the whole of December. I turn as Danielsen and Atii approach the podium and I wave to Aron that I will be with him in a moment.

"Nice speech, ma'am," Atii says.

"Thank you. It's good to have you back. Now, what are you going to do about Gaba?"

"Ma'am?"

"He seems duty-bound to sleep on my couch."

"*Aap*, we talked about that."

"And?"

"He stays until we catch the Calendar Man," Atii says. "No discussion."

"Atii…"

She shakes her head. "It's either Gaba or Danielsen."

I start to say something but stop as soon as Atii starts to laugh.

"I think it's best I stay with the task force, ma'am," Danielsen says. "If you don't mind."

"That'll be fine." I can see he has something else to say. "Aqqa?"

"I checked your schedule with Aron. I just want to be sure you are staying in the office today."

"Yes. Although I plan on voting around lunchtime."

"They say that will be the busiest time, ma'am," Aqqa says with a frown.

"Yes," I say. "Will it be Nikolaj, again?"

"And whoever else I can find."

Danielsen swears under his breath, but he hasn't tried to stop me, and I take that as an encouraging sign. With Gaba's security guards, extra police officers on duty, and the Dutch constabulary pulling double shifts, there is a uniform of one description or another on almost every corner, at the door of every public and vulnerable building, and beside every voting booth. Even the First Minister has noticed, and I think of her public address on the radio at breakfast as Danielsen calls for Aron to join us.

"I want you to stay with the Commissioner all day."

"Alright."

"Nikolaj will be with you too.

"Yes, Sergeant."

"You never leave her side," Danielsen says, with a glance at me.

It would almost be endearing if it wasn't so frustrating. But I'm still on a high following the assembly. I can't remember the last time I spoke to the whole department. It feels good. The whole day feels good, and I take a step back to send a message to Iiluuna, to coordinate our vote. I realise we haven't talked about what we actually want. Thoughts of an independent Greenland, many years ago, were plagued with poisonous agendas that split the country. For Greenlanders such as me, who never learned to speak Greenlandic, our place in our own country, culture and society was questioned. Those were dark times, plagued by corruption at a local and government level. David was stubbornly apolitical, and I remember that it infuriated me. But I wonder what he would have voted for today, if he had the chance.

"Commissioner?" Aron says, and I realise we are alone.

"Yes, Aron."

"Perhaps we could go to your office? I have a few things you need to look at – before you vote."

"Lead the way," I say, but I am slow, as I have to check Iiluuna's message. Aron holds the elevator and I step in beside him. "Two o'clock," I say. "That's when we'll vote. At the community centre opposite the supermarket."

"Is that safe, ma'am?"

"What do you mean?"

"It was the place the Calendar Man left the first body," he says, with a glance at my hands.

"And probably more secure than the police station right now. See how quiet it is."

The desks in the outer office are empty and dark except for a lamp on Aron's desk. The Christmas Stars in the window cast a red glow into the room, and I hesitate to flick the switch for the main lights. It's not often you can call a police station pretty, but there is a thick layer of snow on the window ledges, and flowers of frost on the glass. The administration staff has done their best to compete with the other departments and units, and I see, for what feels like the first time, the effort they have made to decorate the office, and to spread a little Christmas cheer.

Only one thing is missing.

I can't see a single advent calendar on any of the desks.

We have more than enough in the evidence room, I think.

But with only eight days until Christmas, it's beginning to feel festive, as if Christmas will come despite the Calendar Man and his best efforts to ruin it, for me, for the people of Nuuk, and for Greenland.

"It must be ten o'clock," I say.

"I'll make coffee," Aron says, as he dumps the files on his desk. "Unless you want tea, ma'am?"

"Coffee will be perfect, thank you."

It occurs to me that Danielsen has let him off the hook, and that the young man's supposed infatuation, is nothing more than genuine loyalty and concern. Nothing more dangerous than that.

"Sit with me, Aron," I say, as he brings the coffee and rolls into my office. "The paperwork can wait for a moment. Let's just sit for a minute." I pull out a chair and gesture for Aron to do the same. "Tell me about yourself. You arrived during a difficult time for me – David got really sick just after the summer. I feel as though you have been here forever, but I forget it is just a few months, really. Tell me where you come from, and what you will do for Christmas?"

It's a classic case of too much, too soon. Aron splashes the coffee on the table as he pours, and I pull my hand back quickly to avoid hot splashes of coffee on my skin.

"Aron?"

"Sorry, ma'am," he says. He settles once the coffee is poured.

"Christmas?" I say, with a gentle smile.

"With *anaana*, my mum. In Sisimiut."

"Just the two of you?"

Yes," he says. "I never knew my dad, and my sister committed suicide when I was twelve."

"I'm sorry," I say.

It's a sad story, but all too familiar. Suicide clouds nearly every family in Greenland, leaving few untouched, and far too many missed.

"We've accepted it now," he says. "I have, at least."

Aron is quiet for a moment and we sip our coffee. When I put my mug down, I see that one of the Christmas Stars is glowing brighter than before. The red and orange light flickers upon the glass, and the flowers of frost are lit with golden threads. I'm amazed at the detail, the magic of Christmas. I want a closer look, but the pounding of feet in the hallway and the crash of someone slapping the door to one side as they charge into the office dispels the last of the Christmas cheer with a crash of metal and wood as the door slams into the wall and the glass in my office window shakes.

Aron spills his coffee as he reaches for the pistol holstered at his waist, and then he stops, and we both stare at Nikolaj as he slows outside my office. He must have taken the stairs, and he takes a few quick breaths before speaking.

"It's the parliament building," he says, and points towards the Christmas Stars in the windows. "There's a fire. A big one. We have to evacuate."

"Evacuate?"

"We're too close. They want us out."

"Where are we going?" I ask, as I grab my jacket.

"Danielsen is setting up a command centre in the sports hall."

"A command centre? Nikolaj," I say, as I grab his arm. "What's going on?"

"More fires, all over the city."

"How many?"

"Three, maybe four."

"The voting centres?"

"Yes." Nikolaj guides me to the stairs. "We have to go, ma'am. Nuuk is burning."

Pingasunngorneq

Wednesday, 17th December 2042

Chapter 17

The latest reports come in after midnight, by which time the voluntary fire service confirms that the fire at the government building is under control, and that we can return to the police station in the next few hours or wait until mid-morning when it will be safer. We've been here all night, and the grey light of dawn is pressing against the windows of the sports hall. I stand to one side as Danielsen receives reports and updates from across the city.

"Ooqi is offline," he says to me during a brief lull.

"That's unusual."

More than that, I think. *It's unheard of.*

"His activity icon has gone dark. Maybe he was thrown off the server when we evacuated the police station. I don't know." Danielsen sighs as he sees the Chinese representative, Tan Yazhu, walking towards us.

"I'll talk to him," I say. "Just get Ooqi back online."

Tan Yazhu meets me in the middle of the sports hall and we find a place to sit along one of the walls. There is some glitter left over from the Christmas market on the table and I brush it to one side with my hand as Tan Yazhu sits down.

"We are very sorry about the vote," he says.

Initial reports suggest that no-one was hurt at any of the fires at the voting centres, but that voting was disrupted, and the decision of Greenland's independence has been postponed. A brief article I read in *Oqaasaq*, stated that if Greenland doesn't vote before the end of the year, it will be another two years before Denmark will be willing for them to have another referendum. I don't pretend to understand the politics, but I know the fallout will be great, and I feel sad for my country and my people.

"Thank you," I say.

"And the fires. We are sorry for you about them too."

"Yes. But they are under control now. I understand you sent a team of miners to help. We appreciate that."

"*Shì*." Tan Yazhu bows his head. "You're welcome."

"How can I help you?"

"This Calendar Man. Do you think you can catch him?"

His question makes me hesitate for a second. I suppose I have never imagined that we wouldn't, that it was only a matter of time. But perhaps time is running out. If this was the Calendar Man's final act, to prevent the vote from happening, then he could just disappear. Perhaps we will never catch him. I can almost feel the tattoos on my fingers burning and I realise that I want him caught, at all costs.

"Yes," I say. "We will catch him."

"When?"

"That's difficult to say, Tan Yazhu."

"Before Christmas?"

"Ideally, I would like to catch him tonight, but I don't know…"

"Before December twenty-three."

"I don't know."

"It's important, lady Commissioner. December twenty-three is *Dongzhi*. The Winter Solstice. It is very important to us. There will be big celebrations in

Chinatown. Already, the Dutch have missed *Sinterklaas*. Ruined with a monster man left in the administration building. We do not want this to happen to *Dongzhi*. The miners have been working very hard, very hard all year, and they need *Dongzhi*. It is very important. I have promised them everything will be alright. Now you must promise me."

"I cannot promise anything."

"Then we will take matters into our own hands. And you must step aside."

He folds his arms across his small chest. He is smaller than me, smaller than a lot of Greenlanders, but the intensity in his eyes, the way he looks at me, makes him seem twice as tall. Dangerous and committed.

"Tan Yazhu," I say. "You are the Chinese security representative."

"*Shì.*"

"And your official title?"

"That's not important. I am the boss. I am responsible." He stabs the table with his finger. "I will find this man, if you cannot."

"Perhaps we can find him together? I'm sure if we shared our information, then maybe we could help each other."

"Sharing information? Is that what you call hacking our computer?"

I was afraid of this. Ooqi had warned me, but with no communication from the Chinese, zero cooperation, they left me with little choice and I turned a blind eye to Ooqi's search for information. I could even deny it, and I try.

"Could you be more specific, Tan Yazhu?"

"How about this?"

He places a small disc on the table. I recognise it instantly. Although, on closer inspection, the Chinese symbols I saw on the disc the Jonkheer gave me are missing.

"It is a bugging device. I found it in the crack between the leg and surface of my desk. Can you explain?"

"No, I can't."

I really can't. I'm tempted to look at Danielsen, to see if he has established contact with Ooqi, but I think it's best to play ignorant. It's not difficult.

Tan Yazhu stands up and I realise the meeting is about to end.

"You catch him before December twenty, or I will."

"Tan Yazhu…"

"No, lady Commissioner, say nothing more. Just catch him."

"It would help if you shared information about the dead miner. We can use that to help us find the Calendar Man."

Tan Yazhu waves his hand, as if it is irrelevant.

"He was drunk. He died in his apartment. Choked on his own vomit. I sent his body back to China. Good riddance. He was bad worker."

"Thank you," I say, as I think about the opportunistic nature of the Calendar Man. Or was it just a coincidence and the apartment – number nine – was just a number, nothing more.

Tan Yazhu barely even nods before marching with short urgent strides to the entrance. I watch him leave and consider the diplomatic implications of being caught snooping on the Chinese, and the more pressing concern about Tan Yazhu carrying out his own investigation to catch the Calendar Man. I don't want to imagine the methods he might employ, but I can't help wondering if they might produce results, faster and more conclusive than our own.

A shout and a series of quick commands from Danielsen pull me back to the moment, and I watch as the SRU team run towards the door. Danielsen follows at a slower pace and I catch him before he leaves the sports hall.

"What's going on?"

"We've got a sighting, ma'am. A positive identification. Two officers are chasing a man with a backpack towards the docks. I have three police cars en route and the SRU…"

"I'm coming with you," I say. "No discussion. Let's go."

I reach the door of the SRU vehicle before Danielsen, and the team of four heavily-armed officers make space for me in the middle of the passenger area, as Danielsen climbs into the seat beside the driver. The driver accelerates onto the road as the men shut the doors.

"Suspect is medium height," Danielsen says from the front seat. "Medium build. Carrying a black backpack. He's wearing tan coloured work gloves and has a wool hat."

The men wait until Danielsen has finished speaking before they make a last check of their gear, apologising as they bump padded shoulders with me as the driver slings the SRU vehicle around the bends, drifting across the ice before accelerating along the straight sections, siren wailing, lights flashing.

David loved this – the speed, the lights, the excitement and the adrenaline. He pretended he didn't, but I could see it in his eyes every time a patrol car raced past us on the streets. It was even more evident in the final months before he died, when our walks were precious, and he savoured everything he could including the sights, sounds and smells of Greenland's rapidly expanding city. I wish he was here now, and I'm ready for him to just appear on the seat beside me, flashing a toothy grin and gripping my hand at all the excitement. But the man beside me is all but hidden beneath his helmet, behind the mask. I can't see his face, and neither can I pretend he is David. But just one word could make all the difference. David's voice, the one inside my head.

Focus, Piitalaat.

Apparently, I can conjure him on command, and I smile as I kid myself that David's ghost is with me, travelling right beside me as we fly down Nuuk's streets and the driver downshifts the gears and slows at the top of the slope leading down to the docks. There is a bump and a curse as the vehicle shimmies into a snowdrift, followed by a gasp of cold air as the four-man team open the doors on each side of the vehicle and race down the street towards a police officer waving his arms and pointing towards the rocks to the right of the road.

"That way," he shouts. "Fifty metres."

"Ma'am," Danielsen says, as I leap out of the vehicle.

I haven't worn a pistol for over a year, and I feel naked all of a sudden. The thought chills me more than the bite of cold air that tickles my skin and freezes my breath onto the tips of my hair. I can feel the cold pinch my cheeks as I race after the SRU team. I'm almost giddy, invigorated by the pursuit.

Danielsen won't catch me, his midriff and the ice coating the rocks will slow him down. I don't care about slipping. I can hear the SRU team begin to shout, ordering the suspect to get down and stay down. I press the soles of my boots into the prints left by the team in the snow. I can see them now, their submachine guns pointed down at a man on the ground, his black clothes, backpack, and hat dusted with snow. I arrive just as the team leader presses his knee onto the man's back, secures his wrists with plastic shackles, and pulls the man onto his knees.

"Just a minute, ma'am," one of the SRU officers says, as he steps in front of me, slowing me down and shielding me from the suspect. "We need to make sure he's alone."

He is. I'm sure of it.

I nod, and then step to one side. I need to see his face. But I can feel the cold pinch my brow as I see the man – younger than I imagined him to be, with the wispy beard and bushy black eyebrows so typical of Greenlanders.

"It's not him," I say, as Danielsen wheezes to a stop behind me.

"We need to talk to him," he says, between gasps of breath.

"He can't help us."

"We don't know that."

I'm disappointed. Perhaps it is the anti-climax of the chase, the adrenaline evaporating from my body, drawing the heat from my head, and turning my hair white with breath and dismay. I thought we had him. I thought it was over.

I walk away, back towards the road, convinced that we have been on yet another elaborate wild goose chase, with little to show for it. I was so eager, and I wonder if it was because of Tan Yazhu, or the referendum, or just the simple fact that I want this to end so that Nuuk, and me, can get through the darkest month of the year, and just enjoy Christmas. I want to spend Christmas Eve with Iiluuna and Quaa, to watch them open their presents, give them something to show how much they mean to me, and how much they have helped me through my grief.

But no. It was all for nothing. The hunt is still on, and we are desperate for leads.

"Ma'am," Danielsen says, as he catches up to me. His breathing is normal now, but his cheeks are rosy red, complementing the flash of blue emergency lights.

"I'm sorry, Aqqa. I thought we had him."

"We might still," he says. Danielsen pauses to take a breath. "He has a message, from the Calendar Man."

Sisamanngorneq

Thursday, 18th December 2042

Chapter 18

There is no darkness, only ignorance. The Calendar Man's message was the first, the last and the only thing the man told us. Danielsen interviewed him through the night while the city held its breath. If I look out of the office window, I can see the charred façade of the government buildings. I can hear about the fire on the radio or read it in the first few pages – streaming and paper editions – of *Oqaasaq*. I imagine Qitu steering his reporters along different avenues of inquiry, exploring leads and receiving tips as the people of Nuuk weigh in on the activity of the past few days. Gaba wrote a report for the First Minister and sent me a copy. I skimmed the summary with my first coffee of the day, but I am distracted, and I feel the need to look at the evidence again. The paperwork can wait.

"Aron," I say, as I stand at the door to my office. "Can you find Natuk and tell her to meet me in the evidence room."

"Yes, ma'am."

He hesitates, and I know why. It's the end of year budget approval that I have been ignoring, along with several other administrative tasks that need a final signature or a few lines of comments and amendments. I would like to think that these things can wait, but I know that I'm just pushing them, one day at a time.

"I know about the budget," I say. "I promise to look at it later."

What Danielsen and I thought might have been an unhealthy infatuation, turns out to be one of Aron's endearing qualities – a sense of loyalty and responsibility. It will get the better of him one day, I'm sure of it. But one more day won't kill him, and I have other things to deal with, at the personal request of the First Minister. Her voice follows me back into my office as I open a new search page on my browser. There's still no sign of Ooqi, although Danielsen assures me he is looking into it. He is probably exhausted. I don't remember seeing him take a break or a day off. He is always online or at his desk. But without him, I have to do some of the leg work myself.

Danielsen plugged the message into a search engine almost as soon as the man in custody said it. Some of the results were random, others were Shakespearian. He was never on the Greenlandic school curriculum, but the Danes know a little about him. I remember Hamlet having something to do with Denmark, and then there is the Ombudsman's fascination with Shakespeare.

Danes and Shakespeare.

I leave the browser open as I look through the few shelves on the wall of my office. I slipped the Ombudsman's book somewhere between books on law and conduct after a glance at the back cover suggested it would be just as interesting. I don't read books. I know few Greenlanders that do. David was an exception to the rule, but I don't remember him ever reading Shakespeare. I pull the thin volume off the shelf and read the title: *Twelfth Night: Or, What You Will.*

I feel a slight thrill, a subtle crackle of energy in the air as I remember Danielsen's notes, something about the quote. He thinks it could be related to *Twelfth Night*, and he found it in Act IV, Scene II. The message is paraphrased, but clear to see, spoken by a clown and a character called Malvolio. It means nothing to me, but when Aron confirms that Natuk is on her way I take the book with me to the evidence room.

It's curious that the Ombudsman should have an interest in Shakespeare, and that the Calendar Man's message is taken from the very play she suggested I read.

"It's a Christmas story," she had said.

I prefer something cosier, and in a language I understand, but Shakespeare has a new-found meaning, and if it can give us a lead then, no matter how archaic the language, I'm going to have to read it. Of course, if David was alive, I could have asked him to read it to me, as I curled into his body.

Focus, Piitalaat.

"I will," I say, as I scan my thumb and open the door to the evidence room. "I promise."

Natuk is waiting at the table, studying the calendars. I smile as she turns, and I am reminded of a younger version of myself. She has the same oversized police jacket, the boots that give her at least one more inch in height, and the soft eyes that have seen too much suffering already, and yet not so much that the light is fading into shadow. She has a keen mind too, and I want to put it to work.

"We need to start again," I say. I press the book into Natuk's hands and gather up the letters printed on squares of paper beneath each calendar. "Imagine that it has nothing to do with me. We've spent too much time on that already."

"Ma'am?"

"Misdirection. I think we leaped at the chance to

find meaning in Piita's body. Following that line of inquiry just got us stuck in the mud. We need to think differently, attack this differently."

"And the book?" Natuk says, as she turns it in her hands. "Shakespeare?"

"The Ombudsman, Anna Riis, lent it to me. Danielsen thinks the message from the Calendar Man might have come from there. Act four, scene two: *There is no darkness, only ignorance.*"

"I've found it," Natuk says. "Sort of. It's not a direct quote, ma'am."

"No. it's not. But if we imagine it is relevant," I say, and gesture at the calendars. "How does it apply to these?" I smile at the furrow deepening on Natuk's brow. "That's why you're here. Have a think about it, and I'll call Aron for some coffee."

It could be an abuse of power, but Aron was with me when Anna Riis gave me the book. If I ask him to bring coffee, I might jog his memory. It feels good to be contributing again to the investigation. Danielsen is occupied with the interview and Atii is sifting through the crime scenes. With no sign of Ooqi, the task force has been diluted. So, the budget can wait, and I can reassign assets such as Natuk and Aron.

Aron responds to my text, and I slip my mobile into my pocket, standing quietly beside Natuk as she flips through the pages of *Twelfth Night*. She stops after five minutes, takes a closer look at the calendar, and taps her finger on her bottom lip.

"Natuk?"

"There are five calendars," she says.

"Yes."

"There are five acts in the play."

"One calendar for each act?"

"I thought so, but then the number for each window is wrong."

"In what way?"

Natuk flips through the pages of the book and turns it towards me.

"There are five scenes in the first two acts, four in the third, three in the fourth and only one in the fifth."

"And those numbers in the margin. What are they?"

I turn at the sound of Aron struggling to enter the evidence room and carry the tray of coffee, mugs and breakfast rolls. I don't have to look at my watch to know it is ten o'clock, or thereabouts. I leave Natuk with the calendars and help Aron come through the door.

"Thank you, ma'am," he says.

He puts the tray down to one side of the calendars and turns to leave.

"While you're here, Aron," I say. "Why don't you help us a little? The budget can wait."

"If you're sure?"

"That's a loaded question," I say. "How about you give me half an hour of your time, and I'll do the same."

"Alright," he says.

The sight of Aron relaxing makes me feel guilty, as if half an hour of my time is more than he could have hoped for. Since he arrived, I have been preoccupied with David's illness, followed by grief, and now a case that has had me at odds with my staff, and under house arrest. It's a wonder he has managed to get anything signed or processed since he began work as my assistant. But he has a keen mind behind that mask of worry and concern. He could be as sharp as Natuk, if given half the chance. According to our deal, he has half an hour.

Aron leans over the book and traces the lines with the tip of his finger. "The numbers," he says, "correspond to the lines. They are line numbers, that's all."

"It's that simple?"

"Yes, ma'am."

Natuk steps closer to the table and lays the book flat on the surface. She turns the pages to the first act as Aron and I join her at the table.

"Calendar one is Act one," she says. "Do we agree?"

"We do," I say.

"The first window was sixteen, and line sixteen is…"

"*Will you go hunt, my lord?*" Aron reads. "Spoken by Curio. Who's that?"

Natuk flips to the character list at the front of the book.

"An attendant to the Duke. Gentleman. Male."

The way she says it, it sounds like a brief profile of a suspect, and I catch myself smiling. Perhaps there's a reason Shakespeare isn't required reading at the Police Academy.

"How about the second calendar," I say. "What does that give us?"

Natuk turns the book towards Aron as he makes a note on his tablet. He finds the task force server and shares it to the case folder.

"Act two, line nine," Natuk says, as she turns the pages. "*Let me yet know of you whither you are bound,*" she reads. "And that makes no sense."

"It might not have to," I say. "Keep going."

"Act three, line twenty." She pauses and shows the book to Aron.

"What's wrong?" I ask.

"The line starts and finishes on the lines above and below. Do we take the whole sentence?"

"No," Aron says and presses his finger onto the page. "Just take this bit. It makes the most sense."

"...*indeed, words are very rascals*," Natuk reads. "That makes *sense* to you?"

I let them argue for a moment as I step away from the table. The concertina cupboards of the evidence room allow for plenty of space to wander, unless they are in use. I pour a cup of coffee, blowing on the surface as I think about the words, the very rascals. It's a stretch, but the first quote from the first calendar makes some sense – the beginning of the hunt for the Calendar Man. Is he goading us? He wouldn't be the first. If it is aimed at us, then the second quote fits too, as he wonders where we are going, what leads we are following. I wonder if he knew just how confused we were, and, if that is the case, then he is mocking us with the quote from the third calendar, as the words lead us nowhere. Or perhaps he means the evidence, or even the motive. We were focused on me, then back to the referendum. But we had no idea that he was communicating with us, that he had opened an avenue of dialogue – the calendars were less about days and more about communication. But what is he saying?

"What is he saying in calendar four?"

"*Saying*, ma'am?" Natuk says.

"The line, the quote. What is it?"

"*Will you make me believe that I am not sent for...*," she says. "The clown said it. Is it important who says it?"

"It could be."

But I'm not worried about that. This line is more direct. More sinister. On one level, it suggests that what he is doing is justified, and, on another, that he is here at someone's request. But who? Someone from my past? I don't want to go there. What if it is bigger than him, or he *thinks* it is bigger than him. Does he think Greenland *sent* for him? Or is it Denmark?

"The last calendar is another fragment," Natuk says. "...*my friends, and the better for my foes...*"

I hear Aron tap the last quote into his tablet with soft thuds of his fingers on the glass, and Natuk closes the book with a snap. It was the last calendar, his last words of communication before the referendum and the message delivered by his courier.

There is no darkness, only ignorance.

Is ignorance better than darkness? Are things better now that the referendum is postponed? It will be if it is not held before the end of the year. Is that the result the Calendar Man intended, to put things off for at least another two years?

If the calendars are meant to be interpreted, and we have done it right this time, then the Calendar Man has been sending messages from day one. It's time we sent one back.

Tallimanngorneq

Friday, 19th December 2042

Chapter 19

"I'm sorry we couldn't meet yesterday," Pipaluk says, as she welcomes me into her suite at Hotel Hans Egede. "It's been hectic, and we're still trying to discover what we have lost, since the fire."

"It's only been three days," I say. "I understand completely."

"Do you?" she says, as she sits down.

She seems sterner than usual, with a more aggressive cut of her clothes that extends to the straight and firm set of her jaw. I decide it is the shock of the fire and the failed referendum and let her comment pass.

"I've seen the fire chief's report. He says you should be able to move back into your office before Christmas."

"I've seen it too. The fire was superficial. The walls are a bit black on the outside, but the damage is irreparable."

"You mean the referendum?"

"Is there anything else more important at the moment, Commissioner?" Pipaluk clenches her fists and presses them on the table as she leans towards me. "I asked you to see to this case, personally, Petra. That was all. And yet, you deferred to some Sergeant from one of the settlements."

"Sergeant Danielsen has an exemplary record, First Minister."

"That's touching. He no doubt holds you in the same high regard, which is why he wasted time protecting you, and let this Calendar Man run riot through the town and tear down the foundations of Greenland's future with a few dead bodies and a handful of advent calendars."

I honestly thought this meeting was going to be better than this, but I had forgotten how important the question of Greenlandic independence is for Pipaluk Uutaaq, how personal it is for her and her family – the living and the dead.

"Sergeant Danielsen was reacting to the information we had at the time."

"Information interpreted by your own officers." Her heels bite into the carpet as she stands up and walks to the window. She stands close to the glass and stares down at Nuuk's main street. "This is our country," she says, her voice almost a whisper. "I don't think you understand how important it is to be allowed to govern what is ours, to make our own mistakes. I've met people in the small towns who are ready to work two, maybe even three jobs if they think it will make a difference, if it might help the economy – our economy. We've been under the Danish thumb for far too long. And now these climate immigrants…" She turns to look at me. The sneer on her lips is as sharp as ice. "It's just another colonial foothold, reminding us that we had better tow the line, do as *they* say. That we will never make it on our own."

"I thought you signed off on the Dutch agreement?"

"I signed it; I didn't *sign off*, Petra. There's a difference."

"But the money that they pay to the state…"

"Is just another grant, a lump sum to keep us content. It should have made us better off, but the Danes just adjusted their contribution to allow for it. We're no richer, no poorer, and no closer to economic independence."

"That's not what you said," I say.

"No?" Pipaluk laughs. "After all you've been through, Petra, after all these years, I never expected you to be so naïve. But then, you are the token Greenlander in a very public position. What? That surprises you too? You're a political pawn, Petra. Just like me."

Perhaps I have been naïve, but when I was encouraged to apply for the position of Police Commissioner, I honestly thought it was the natural step up the ladder after many years of service on the force. I managed to distance myself from the politics, and maybe that was my first mistake.

It is time to make amends.

"Earlier," I say, "you asked me if I understand. I think what you really want to ask me is how I would have voted, if I had had the chance."

Pipaluk crosses her arms as she waits by the window. Her jaw has softened, only a little, but enough to reveal her curiosity. She wants to know. And I'm ready to tell her.

"I would have voted *yes*," I say. "Yes, for an independent Greenland. Does that surprise you?"

"Honestly, it does."

"Because I don't speak Greenlandic."

She laughs. "You're confusing me with my father. I don't care what language you speak, Petra. But I didn't think you would vote for independence, because I don't think you want to fight." She raises her hand as I start to speak. "Don't mistake me. I know you're strong, and you've had your battles, tougher than anything I have experienced. But I think you're ready to stop. To let life continue on around you. I think you're looking for peace, something you've earned, but a vote for independence is not the peaceful choice. It's going to be tough, and I didn't think you wanted to fight."

"Then we have something in common, First Minister."

"What's that?"

"We both underestimate each other."

I stand up and walk to join her at the window. The midmorning sky is lightening, and the Northern Lights are barely visible. This city, taller than it once was, has grand ambitions. She's not wrong, I do want a peaceful life, but I don't think I'll ever stop fighting. Not really. I pull a folded piece of paper from my pocket and press it into her hands.

"What's this?"

"Something I want you to work into your speech."

"My speech?" she asks, as she frowns at the words I have written on the paper.

"The one when you announce a new referendum, on the twenty-third of December."

"The night before Christmas Eve? It can't be done."

"I think it can. You just need to convince your staff." I smile as the frown ruins her otherwise perfect composure. "What was it you said? Something about people doing two or three jobs to make things work, to achieve an independent Greenland. A new referendum won't make that a certainty, but it will give the people of Greenland a chance to do something about it, to fight for it – with their voice, of course. They will be heard."

"And the Calendar Man? He's achieved his goal.

Won't this just incite him?"

I tap the paper in her hand.

"You're going to send him a message, First Minister."

"*Be not afraid of greatness*?"

"And the next bit," I say.

"*Fate, show thy force.*" Pipaluk folds the paper into her pocket. "What message, exactly, am I sending, Commissioner?"

"You're calling him out, so that we can catch him."

"I'm not just painting a target on my chest?"

"You've had one from the day you entered office, First Minister. I don't think a few more days are going to make a difference."

"I suppose not."

I leave her by the window. How she works Shakespeare into her speech is up to her and her staff. How I catch the Calendar Man is up to me.

I smile at Nikolaj as I open the suite door, and we walk quietly along the carpeted corridor to the elevator. Gaba's security guards are everywhere. I nod at one of them as Nikolaj presses the button for the elevator and the door opens.

"You're not coming with me?" I ask, as he waits in the corridor.

"Natuk will meet you in reception. I've been assigned to the First Minister." Nikolaj can't quite hide the smile on his lips. "Better hours," he says, as the door closes.

I should warn him about the sleepless nights Pipaluk has ahead of her, but I have a childish urge to giggle instead, and I allow myself that little pleasure from the top floor to reception.

Piitalaat.

"I know," I say, as the elevator bell rings once prior to the doors opening. "I'll behave. I promise."

"What's that, ma'am," Natuk says, as I walk out of the elevator.

"Nothing important. Let's go back to the station."

"We can't," she says, as she opens the door of the SUV parked at the entrance. "Danielsen needs you to see something."

"What?"

"It's best you see for yourself," she says, and closes the passenger door.

It's hard not to feel optimistic when the sun shines in the winter in Greenland. The towns, villages and settlements further north won't see the sun for another few weeks, longer in Qaanaaq at the very top of Greenland, but Nuuk and the south enjoy lower latitudes. I pull down the sun visor as Natuk accelerates.

"He said it was urgent, ma'am," she says, when I glance at the speedometer.

I'm curious and tempted to suggest we turn on the emergency lights and siren. For David's sake, of course. Although, the smile on Natuk's face suggests she is not immune to the thrill of a rapid response.

"It's nearly Christmas, Natuk. There are a lot of people about."

"Ma'am?"

"Turn on the siren. It will be safer."

And more fun for Natuk, I think, as she pushes the new electric SUV to an appropriate, if slightly elevated speed. I glance at the graveyard and send a thought to David as we flash past it.

The fun stops as Danielsen waves us over to the side of the road and Natuk parks beside the SRU patrol vehicle in the parking area below one of Nuuk's older residences – a grey apartment block devoid of Christmas Cheer.

"Danielsen?" I say, as I tug at the collar of my jacket and join him by the side of the SRU vehicle. The four SRU officers are wearing body armour and ballistic helmets. Their submachine guns are trained on the windows of the building, and a quick glance to the left and right reveals more officers in armour in strategic positions. The building is surrounded.

"You've found him?" I say, and I clench my fingers inside my jacket pockets as they begin to tremble.

"*Naamik*," Danielsen says. "It's not him."

"Then who?"

"Atii responded to a call this morning. Four men armed with what could be Chinese bangsticks."

"I don't know what they are."

"Basically, a simple explosive device at the end of a rod, that can be fitted with charges or other attachments. Harpoons, for example. The men inside the building were seen carrying at least two each. Atii is inside negotiating, but they won't come out. One of the men says you promised him something. And, according to him, you have the rest of the day to do it."

"Who is she talking with?"

"Tan Yazhu," Danielsen says. "He says you promised to catch the Calendar Man before the twentieth of December. And if you don't, then he and his men will carry out their own investigation, starting at dawn tomorrow."

"But they're surrounded."

"I don't think that was part of the plan, ma'am."

"We don't have time for this," I say.

I imagine that Pipaluk will arrange a live interview on the early evening news. As soon as she makes it known that there will be a new referendum, the Calendar Man will be forced to act.

"We can't have our men tied up here," I say.

"I agree, ma'am." Danielsen tugs the radio from the clip on his jacket. "Atii has been briefed about the First Minister's speech and the new referendum. She knows what to do."

"She's ready to go in?"

Danielsen nods.

I wonder if this is what the First Minister imagined when she wondered if I was ready to fight for my country? Coupled with the thought that I am a Danish-speaking Greenlander in a very visible public office, I am tempted to call her, and postpone the announcement. But that would mean postponing the referendum and sabotaging a last attempt to allow the people to vote for their future. The towns, villages and settlements outside Nuuk might have escaped the Calendar Man's campaign of terror, but turnout to the polls was limited by the drama playing out on the radio and streaming media. The digital booths could be reset, but the people still had to visit them.

"Ma'am?"

"This might be my last order as Police Commissioner," I say.

"It might." Danielsen lowers his hand, the stubby radio antennae scratches against the rough weave of his trousers. "It might also be the most important."

"What would you do, Aqqa?"

"Me?"

"You might be in this same position one day. What would you do?"

"In the same situation? A terrorist on the loose a few days before a new referendum to vote on our independence, when foreign investment will play a critical role in our economic future."

"Yes."

"And you're about to storm a building to pacify four armed foreign nationals, whose country is one of Greenland's greatest investors."

"That's about the size of it, Aqqa," I say. "What would you do?"

He laughs. It's contagious.

"*Be not afraid of greatness*," he says. "Apparently, that's Shakespeare. Whoever he was."

"I prefer the other line," I say. "*Fate, show thy force.*"

And in that moment, I know what I have to do.

"Tell Atii to keep negotiating."

"And if it doesn't work?"

"You go in at dawn," I say. "That's an order."

Arfininngorneq

Saturday, 20th December 2042

Chapter 20

Natuk picks me up one hour before dawn. In the north of Greenland dawn is still months away. For Tan Yazhu and his team of three security guards, we chose four o'clock in the morning. I need the SRU team and rest of the department rested and ready to respond to the Calendar Man's reaction to the First Minister's announcement. To put it bluntly, the Chinese are in my way. Regardless of politics and international relations, it is bad timing.

Natuk is quiet as we drive. I turn on the radio, hear a repeat of the closing remarks of the First Minister's speech, and smile at the familiar words.

"That could be a first, you know," I say.

"What's that, ma'am?"

"A Greenlandic politician quoting Shakespeare."

Natuk says nothing more until we can see the police cordon around the grey concrete residence. She parks beside Danielsen's patrol car.

"I'm worried about Ooqi," she says. "No-one has seen him. He hasn't called in."

"Perhaps he has taken a day off. He's been working all week."

I should know, or at least find out, but I am distracted. I'm also impatient to get out of the car and be present when the SRU team storm the residence. I reach for the door handle but relax my grip when Natuk speaks.

"I think he's involved in something," she says. "He's been quiet for months now. Ever since the summer. We used to talk. Nothing more than that, but he was pleasant to be around. Now he's quiet and withdrawn."

"Involved in something?"

"Or taking something. Have you noticed that he doesn't look you in the eye?"

"He doesn't say much, but I don't remember thinking he was avoiding me or any of the task force."

"It could be drugs," Natuk says. "I wouldn't have said anything, and I don't want him to get into trouble. But if he's already in trouble, I want to help him."

"Let's find him first. It might just be his day off, and he has gone on a fishing trip in the fjord."

"You don't know Ooqi," she says. "He's too moody to fish. Since the summer, at least."

I should ask more, show a little more support at the very least, but Danielsen has waved twice now. They are ready. He doesn't need a command from me, but I want to be there, to be visible – visibly fighting for Greenland.

"Find him, Natuk. If he needs help, I'll do all that I can."

Natuk stays in the car as I jog to Danielsen's position. He gestures for me to crouch behind a large ballistic shield. The glass in the shield's bulletproof window is sticky with frost and he wipes it clean with his elbow.

"Atii is on the roof with the team making the entry. They will rappel down the sides and enter through the windows. We have units with shields at all the exits."

"And the negotiations failed, I gather."

"Atii tried until early evening. She took a break for a few hours while one of the Danish officers tried a new tack – he said he had some experience, and I thought it couldn't hurt."

"It's fine, Aqqa. I left you in charge."

"Yes, ma'am." He shifts to a more comfortable position. "But it didn't help."

"We're sure they're still inside?"

"Absolutely. There's no way out. We've got the cellar covered and they can't dig through granite." He takes a breath. "They've had their chance, ma'am. Now it's up to the SRU to bring them in without any casualties. They'll use flashbangs."

"And the media?"

"One of Qitu's journalists is on the other side of the cordon, down there," he says and points to a police car at the opposite end of the street. "But I think they are too busy speculating over what will happen now the First Minister has announced a new referendum."

"They're not the only ones."

Danielsen lifts his finger at a double-click from his radio.

"That's it."

I look through the glass and can almost see the rapid descent of three of the SRU officers from the roof to the windows of the apartment the Chinese have occupied. I hear a splinter of glass and I'm blinded by the magnesium flash of light from the windows, and my ears are ringing from three concussive blasts. I can't imagine what it must be like inside the apartment.

The thunder in my ears settles and I hear shouts and cries in Chinese, commands in English, and a muffled explosion.

"Bangstick," Danielsen says.

I worry that the next sound will be the rapid stutter of one of the SRU's silenced submachine guns, but the night is still once more, and then I hear Atii's voice on the radio.

"Four subjects detained," she says. "One injury."

"Who?" Danielsen asks.

"One of the Chinese. A bangstick discharged as he reached for it. I've sent a medic in. It's not life-threatening."

I realise I am holding my breath, and I breathe as Danielsen sends his congratulations to the team. I spare a thought for Aron as I realise the incident might be over, but the paperwork is just about to begin.

"Well, that's it," Danielsen says.

"Have you been here all night?"

"I had a break for a few hours. I came back at midnight."

"I'll send Natuk home, if you'll let me buy you breakfast," I say.

"I'd like that, ma'am."

Natuk hasn't moved, and I see the blue glow of her mobile lighting her face. She starts as I tap on the window.

"I'm sorry," she says. "I thought it was over."

"It is, and I want you to go home. Get some sleep, and then I want you to find Ooqi. You're right to be concerned. Keep me updated."

"I'm your protection, ma'am."

"Sergeant Danielsen is relieving you."

"Okay," she says.

I wait for her to pull away and then join Danielsen in his patrol car. There are more cafés in Nuuk today than there have ever been, which means there are about twelve, and three of them are open all night. Danielsen groans as I suggest we go to *Tupilaq*.

"What's wrong with that?"

"The music," he says. "It's seventies."

"Greenland's favourite soundtrack."

"Yes, ma'am."

Tupilaq has a certain vibe about it, even at five o'clock on a Saturday morning. It is far enough away from Nuuk's bars and nightclubs to put off hungry revellers, but the menu and the very early morning specials, encourage some people to stay up half the night to try *Huevos Rancheros* or *Cowboy Scramble*. The secret is the eggs, and where they get them from. David loved it here, and, when he was in too much pain to sleep, he would dress quietly, leave a note, and slip out of the apartment. I usually caught up with him at the end of the road, pretending that I couldn't sleep, and that breakfast at two in the morning was just what I wanted. It was easier in the summer, when it was light all night. But the winter dark was another matter.

"My treat," I say, as we find an empty table and I gently push thoughts of David to the back of my mind. I'll revisit them later, but, for now, I think I need to repair my relationship with my Sergeant.

"What's good?"

"You've never been?"

I catch myself before I glance at Danielsen's waistline. He takes off his jacket and his uniform blue sweater bulges over his utility belt.

"My wife's cooking," he says and pats his belly. "Good Greenlandic food. I never eat out."

"I thought you had filled out a bit recently."

"*Aap.*"

"Then I'd go for the scrambled eggs, on thick toast. Canadian style."

I order for both of us, and then, as the waitress brings us coffee, I decide to apologise.

"I understand why you might think this case was all about me, Aqqa," I say. "And I'm sorry I gave you a hard time about it."

He sips his coffee, but his eyes never leave mine, and then he raises his eyebrows in a classic Greenlandic *yes*.

"And I'm sorry I went behind your back to the Deputy Commissioner."

"I'm sure I would have done the same," I say.

"Maybe."

The waitress returns with a double order of scrambled eggs on toast, and we say nothing more until we are both finished eating. Danes would have talked the whole way through the meal, but I relish that part of our culture. Somehow, we still manage to hold onto the sacred peace around mealtimes.

But it is technology that disturbs the peace as the waitress refills our coffee mugs. The beep of an incoming message on my mobile seems loud, but after reading it, the second beep feels louder than one of the SRU's flashbangs.

YOU SHOULDN'T HAVE DONE THAT, MA'AM.

"Ooqi? What shouldn't I have done?" I say with a glance at Danielsen.

FATE, SHOW THY FORCE.

"He's quoting Shakespeare," I whisper to Danielsen. "From the First Minister's speech." I hold my mobile closer to my lips. "Where are you, Ooqi?"

YOU DON'T WANT TO KNOW.

"Why? What are you doing?"

YOU DON'T WANT TO KNOW, BUT YOU

WILL, SOON ENOUGH.

"Ooqi," I say. "Listen to me. People are worried about you. Natuk is worried about you. I think you're tired – we're all tired. Tell me where you are. I can come and get you."

YOU SHOULDN'T WORRY ABOUT ME. YOU DON'T HAVE TO THINK ABOUT NATUK.

"Is she with you?" I press the phone to my body and whisper to Danielsen. "I told her to find Ooqi."

Danielsen nods as he stands up and moves away from the table. He pulls out his mobile. *Atii*, he mouths as he dials.

"Ooqi, listen..."

NAAMIK. YOU HAVE TO LISTEN.

A blurred image flickers onto the screen. It sharpens as it increases in size. It's a child, a girl, she's in a kitchen, looking away from the camera, her chin is pointed down, she's laughing, her teeth bright. I recognise the cut of her hair, the glow of her skin. If I could see her soft brown eyes, I know they would be shining with candlelight.

SHE'S IMPORTANT TO YOU?

"Yes," I say, my voice little more than a breath, softer than the beat of my heart, quieter than the blood pulsing through my veins.

THEN STOP THE REFERENDUM.

The screen flickers and he is gone, and he has taken the image of the girl with him.

"Atii is at the station. She'll meet us there," Danielsen says, as he walks to our table. "Ma'am? Petra?"

"We can't go to the station."

"I think it best if we do. We need to dig into Ooqi's background. We need to know everything about him. Then we'll find him, and Natuk."

"He hasn't got Natuk," I say, as I press my hand over my mouth. I turn my head to look at Danielsen, peel my fingers from my lips, and force myself to say it. "It's Quaa. He's got Quaa. You have to take me to Iiluuna. Now, Aqqa. We have to go now."

The next steps are the hardest. From the café to Danielsen's patrol car. I'm on autopilot as he races through the streets. There are no smiles at the swirl of emergency lights, and I can't hear the sirens. I can only see her face – sweet, innocent Quaa, crowned in a wreathe with candles flickering, her bright white teeth flashing. I can feel her weight on my thighs as she eats breakfast. I can smell her hair – coconut shampoo – as she sits beside me and leans over the cookies, decorating them with icing sugar – it's thick, it requires all her concentration to paint it onto the baked dough.

I see and smell all these things, but I taste nothing, my mouth is dry, as I realise that I did this.

This is my fault.

Iiluuna is at the door. Her fingers are white around the door frame as she steadies herself. She lets go when we arrive, and I hold her tight as she shakes until Danielsen suggests we go inside, into the kitchen.

The First Minister wondered if I was strong enough to fight for my country, or would I choose the peaceful alternative. I made a decision then, in her office, when I suggested what to say and another outside the residence before ordering armed police to storm the building. It seems I am good at telling others what to do. As for fighting, when it's personal and the stakes are higher than those on the political and international agenda? That's something else altogether. If the First Minister was here, if she saw me now, I don't think she would question if I was prepared to fight. I don't even think she would recognise me.

Sapaat

Sunday, 21st December 2042

Chapter 21

Danielsen left me with Iiluuna, promising regular updates, and to send someone to pick me up in the morning. I don't remember much of the night, and Ooqi was silent and invisible. The most notable update was when Danielsen informed me he had seconded Aron to the task force. Apparently, my personal assistant has undiscovered talents.

"Ooqi helped me out every now and again," he says, when I arrive at the station. "I paid attention. It wasn't too hard."

"And Ooqi is out of the system now?"

"We can't know that for certain, ma'am," Danielsen says. "It's probably best to assume he still has full access."

"There's nothing we can do?"

Danielsen looks tired, which is to be expected, but there is a spark in his eyes that gives me hope, and it lifts his shoulders a couple of inches.

"Aron thinks we can use it, to mislead him."

"It's an idea," Aron says. "But Ooqi will know that we know he could still be in the system. He will have thought of that." Aron lowers his voice. "He's very clever."

"You looked up to him," I say.

"Yes, ma'am. I'm sorry."

"There's nothing to be sorry about. I confided in Ooqi," I say with a glance at Danielsen. "He had access to the Dutch, and the Chinese – for a limited period. My guess is that he has had access to almost everyone for longer than we can imagine."

"But why?" Danielsen says. "I mean, we know his agenda, but what's his motive?"

"That's what we have to find out," I say. "Aron, I want you to scour the server for everything we know about Ooqi, his personal life and his career. Talk to Natuk. I think she knows more about Ooqi than any of us."

The wall screen flickers behind me as Aron casts clumps of text, scanned documents, images and video clips into a collage of Ooqi's life. I glance at the wall and feel a surge of strength as we begin to compile the most complete profile of the Calendar Man to date. I need every ounce of strength and energy I can muster. I have to be strong for Iiluuna, determined and undaunted for Quaa.

"Aqqa, I know you're tired, but I need you to coordinate the search for Quaa."

"*Aap.*"

"Atii," I say, as she enters the room. "Good work last night."

"Thank you, ma'am."

"I want you to meet with Qitu at NMG. I have a feeling he will have access to information not on our servers. Qitu has made a lot of enemies in the past, and I know his systems are protected, probably better than ours. There's a chance Ooqi has not accessed them. Anything you find might give us an advantage."

I stop for a moment as Aron casts an image of Ooqi onto the screen. He is wearing swimming trunks and standing next to a Greenlandic girl of about the same age, only a little shorter than he is. Their facial features are almost identical. In the background I can see a beach, and what look like red brick buildings on the other side of the dunes. It looks like Denmark.

"Aron, can you send me a copy of that?"

I feel my phone vibrate as Aron shares the image

with my account.

"Where will you be, ma'am?" Atii asks. "If we need to contact you."

"I'm going to visit the Ombudsman, Anna Riis. And, I'd like to borrow your husband."

It's the last advent of Christmas before Christmas Eve and the Ombudsman's house is a picture-perfect example of the Scandinavian wooden house in the snow, red paper stars glowing in the windows, and lanterns pressed into black buckets of sand either side of the thick green door. I can see movement inside the house from the window of Gaba's car.

"Who's the guy," Gaba asks, as he fiddles his glasses out of the case. He pushes them onto the bridge of his nose with the tip of his finger.

"When did you start wearing glasses?"

"Funny, Petra." He stabs a thick finger towards the house. "Who's the man in the kitchen?"

Whoever he is, he's smartly dressed, and I realise it is the Dutch Jonkheer. Ooqi failed to read the Jonkheer's mails to Anna Riis. At least, that's what he told me.

"It's Coenraad Kuijpers. You've seen him before, when we waited outside his office."

"*Aap.*"

"And she showed up, very late."

"Coincidence or something more carnal?"

"His wife passed away. His children are in Denmark. He is probably lonely."

"And how does he know her?"

"She brokered the deal for the climate colony," I say.

Gaba sighs and shifts in his seat, stretching his

long legs and pressing the caps of his boots against the wheel arch.

"Do we wait for him to leave?"

I look at my watch. The short day will turn grey and then black within the hour – one more hour of terror for Quaa. I tug the Ombudsman's copy of *Twelfth Night* from the pocket of my police jacket and open the car door.

"I trust you can convince him to come back later," I say, as I step out of the car.

The snow crunches beneath our boots as we walk to the green door. Gaba holds up his hand for me to wait as I reach for the door knocker. He slips his glasses inside the case and into his pocket and nods.

I take a breath. It's the calm before the storm. I have a theory that the Ombudsman knows something about Ooqi, and I'm hesitant, wondering about the best way to approach her. Gaba takes the initiative, places his hand over mine and lifts the door knocker. He knocks three times, letting go as we hear footsteps on the other side of the door.

"You were dawdling," he says and takes a step back.

"Commissioner Jensen," the Ombudsman says, as she opens the door. "It's Sunday."

"And urgent. Can we come in?"

Anna looks over her shoulder. I can just see the Jonkheer's jacket hanging over the back of one of the kitchen chairs. Her grey hair is tied up neatly, and her cardigan is trim and fashionable, the colours are from the designer winter collection, I remember the catalogue left on our doormat, a few days before I took David to the hospital, and he never left. I give the thought a gentle push out of mind and focus instead on the framed photograph of two young Greenlandic children posing in front of an animal enclosure at the zoo. We don't have any zoos in Greenland, and I'm tempted to compare the picture of the boy and girl with the one Aron sent to my mobile.

"It's really not a good time," she says.

"Yeah, we don't care about that," Gaba says. He leans around me and slaps the door inwards with his arm. "After you, Commissioner."

"This is not acceptable," Anna says, but I am already in the hall, and Gaba is banging the snow from his boots as the Jonkheer steps out of the kitchen.

"Is everything alright, Anna?"

His English is clipped and cultivated, whereas Gaba's is blunt with the potential to get bloody. There's a reason I *borrowed* him from Atii.

"Go back in the kitchen, sit down and shut up, sir," he says.

"You do realise who I am," Anna says.

"You're the one people complain to when they have a beef with the government," Gaba says, as he guides Anna into the living room with a firm grip of her elbow.

"And if you're here in an official capacity…"

"We are," I say, as Gaba helps the Ombudsman into one of two padded armchairs. I sit in the one next to her. Gaba stands in the centre of the room where he can keep an eye on the kitchen. "A girl has been abducted, and I have some questions."

"You can't possibly think that has anything to do with me, Commissioner."

"Perhaps not directly." I press her copy of *Twelfth*

Night onto the arm of her chair. "Why did you lend me that?"

"This is what links me to your missing girl?"

"Just answer the question," Gaba says.

Anna picks up the book and flicks through it. I marked several pages with strips of paper, and they slip out of the pages as she turns them.

"You've read it?"

"I've skimmed it. But you haven't answered the question."

Anna looks at Gaba, and then slowly turns her head to look at me.

"It's a Christmas story," she says. "A comedy – tragic in many respects. A classic. I thought you might enjoy it."

"No," I say. "There's more to it than that. I think you gave it to me for a reason."

"You're digging for something, Commissioner. Why don't you just tell me why you think I gave you the book?"

"So that I could communicate, with the Calendar Man."

Anna closes the book and places it on her lap. She smooths the crease of her wool skirt and then clasps her hands on top of the book. She could be just another well-dressed grandmother if her flint-like eyes didn't spark when I looked at her.

"And did you?" she asks. "Communicate?"

"We tried."

"Not very well, and far too late."

Gaba shuffles his feet and I lift my hand, gesturing for him to stand down. I'm tempted to tell him to wait in the kitchen, but I'm concerned that the Jonkheer might incite him to violence. Gaba is not a violent man, but his strong-handed tactics can be misinterpreted. I already have one international incident to deal with. I don't need another.

"Please explain," I say.

"I don't believe I am required to explain anything. I lent you a book. A seasonal story. That's all."

"And right now, an eight-year-old girl is in danger. That book provides a link to the man who has abducted her, and I think you know who that is. I also think you gave me the book so that I might be able to decipher some of the man's messages, I just don't understand why."

"I'll arrange for you to speak with my lawyers in the morning. You'll have to be up early, of course, their head office is in Denmark."

"We don't have time for this," Gaba says. He takes a step forwards and I meet him halfway, pressing my hand to his chest and shaking my head.

"It doesn't matter," I say, as I turn to look at the Ombudsman. "You've obviously washed your hands of your son. You're abandoning him."

"My son? I don't have a son."

"No? A foster child then. Someone you care about – or pretended to, until he was no longer of use to you."

Anna's frown is so deep it looks like a gash in her forehead. It could be the light casting shadows, but I can see she is starting to crack.

"Coenraad," she says, and I hear the kitchen floorboards creak as the Jonkheer crosses the floor.

"Gaba."

"Got it."

I swear he lives for this, but he has learned, over

the years, to hide his enjoyment, and his smile is thin and unimpressive, unlike the look of shock on the Jonkheer's face as Gaba meets him at the living room door and invites him to go back to the kitchen with a single slap to the chest. Anna starts to rise at the sound of a chair crashing to the floor, but I stop her with a firm grip of her shoulder. I show her the image of the children playing on the beach in Denmark, and she sinks into the armchair, clutching the book to her chest like a shield.

"It's Ooqi, isn't it?"

"Yes," she says, her voice barely a whisper.

"When?"

"The summer of 2026. He was nine."

"And the girl? Who is she?"

"Oh, I think you know her too, Commissioner. Her name is…"

"Natuk," I say, but I can barely hear my voice.

"You think Ooqi is dangerous?" Anna laughs, and lowers the book-shield, just a little. "You wait until you see what she is capable of. Of course, now that her bother is exposed, she'll be gone. You'll never find her, unless she wants you to."

"Brother and sister."

"Yes," Anna says. She puts the book down and beckons for me to follow her to the wall opposite the window. "They came to me when they were both seven years old. They are twins, but you wouldn't know it. Not since puberty. Natuk is so much more mature than her brother, she always has been. Probably due to what her father did to her. Ooqi was lucky, he was only beaten. They were born in Denmark, and they came to me when the social services stepped in. Far too late if you ask me." She points at a picture of a double birthday. "Ah, this was their twelfth," she says. "January 6th, 2019."

"The twelfth night."

"That's right. *Hellige tre konger* or Epiphany if you prefer it in English."

"And you read the book to them?"

"I've always been a Shakespeare fan. Imagine what fun I had trying to explain what the bard was talking about. I mean, Greenlanders are so visual. If you say it's raining cats and dogs they will look outside and call you a liar, but Shakespeare's play on words and multiple hidden meanings and deception… Well, it took a long time for Natuk and Ooqi to understand any of it."

"I think they got the hang of it," I say, as I think of how Ooqi had us running in circles across the city. *And now he has Quaa.*

"Here's another birthday photo," Anna says. "I gave them each a computer that year. They were coding after only two months."

"I'd like you to come with us, back to the station," I say. "We need to find Ooqi, and the little girl, and we need to gain a better understanding of who he is and what motivates him."

"Oh, I can't help you with that, Commissioner. Not until he has finished what he has started. There's far too much at stake."

Ataasinngorneq

Monday, 22nd December 2042

Chapter 22

I don't remember much of the night, only that the sofa in the staff lounge is more comfortable than it used to be, and that Aron's coffee gets stronger by the hour. The Ombudsman said nothing more until just after five o'clock in the morning, the start of a new working day in Copenhagen, four hours ahead of Greenland. Aron woke me to take the call and pressed a mug of coffee into my hand as he guided me into my office.

"Anything new?" I ask, as I slump into my chair.

He shakes his head. I don't think he has slept, and he certainly hasn't been home to change his shirt. Neither have I.

"They're on hold," he says. "Just push the button when you're ready, ma'am."

I'm not ready, but the coffee helps.

I reach for the phone and my hand brushes a note taped to the receiver – something about a meeting with a representative for the Chinese at nine o'clock, Greenlandic time.

"This is Petra Jensen," I say, as I press the handset to my ear. "Police Commissioner." It's almost an afterthought.

"You do realise what you've done?" the lawyer says. I didn't catch his name.

"I've taken Ombudsman Anna Riis into custody in connection with an ongoing case of terror, referendum manipulation and kidnapping."

"You're charging her with *all* that?"

I can hear the lawyer laugh and I grip the phone in my hands.

"I'm interviewing her about *all* that. So far she is

saying nothing."

"And she won't, until she has legal representation."

"We can provide a lawyer."

"She has a lawyer, and you can wait until we get there."

"And when will that be?"

"Two days before Christmas, Commissioner? I think you know the answer to that."

Clearly, he doesn't understand the situation, and neither does he care. I take a breath as I try to formulate a more professional response than the one I want to give him, when Aron appears at the door. I can just see the Jonkheer behind him in the outer office. The lawyer can wait, and I slam the handset onto the receiver.

"The Jonkheer wants to see you, ma'am."

"Let him in," I say, with a brief wave at the table. "And stay with us, Aron."

Aron waits by the door as the Jonkheer smooths the lapels of his jacket with slim hands. His fingers are trembling, and he looks as though he has slept less than I have.

"Commissioner," he says.

"Yes?"

"I need to know what I can expect."

He grips the back of a chair. I think he might fall without it.

"I don't know what you mean."

"I have information, and if I share it, I would like to know if I am... If that will be favourable... If I will be treated favourably, I mean."

"Why don't you sit down," I say.

Aron slips out of the office and brings the

Jonkheer a mug of fresh coffee. It occurs to me that we wouldn't have got through the month without it.

"Thank you," the Jonkheer says.

"Why don't you start again."

"Yes, I'm terribly upset about this. As you know, I am a father. And it was never meant to happen like this. I was assured that no matter how gruesome, no-one would get hurt, and there was never talk of children – never children."

Aron slips his phone onto the table as I sit down opposite the Jonkheer. At a nod from me he presses the record button.

"Are you saying you know what's going on?"

"Yes," he says. "But you must understand. We are in such a precarious position – my countrymen, and I. In desperate times one does unimaginable things. The Netherlands have been under the shadow of climate consequences – climate change – for as long as I can remember. My parents' generation knew it too. Even as we built the Vaalserberg Towers, we knew it was a symbolic gesture, one life raft for a whole nation. That's when we looked to the former colonies, and to other countries willing to take us in. But we were not refugees, not yet. We wanted some assurances, and your government agreed to terms that would allow us not only to relocate huge numbers of our people, but to preserve our culture for future generations with a small village built after our own design."

"This was the deal brokered by Anna Riis?"

"Yes. And it was favourable to us, and the Danes. Perhaps less so to your government. But I was assured it would never be a problem. But in the three years we have been in Greenland, the question of independence has grown to alarming levels. We were so concerned we took steps – through official channels, of course. But since Anna Riis left the government to take up the position as Ombudsman here in Nuuk, our voice was drowned in the Danish government, not unlike our people back home in our shrinking country. But Anna did not desert us. She knows what is best for Greenland, Denmark and my own people."

"What exactly are you saying?"

The Jonkheer glances at Aron's mobile and presses his palms upon the table, gaining strength as he stills the trembling in his fingers.

"Nothing more, until I am sure we can make a trade."

"A trade?"

"I give you information, and you protect me – as a witness."

"What kind of information? More details about the Calendar Man?"

"Yes," he says. "And something more. I know where he girl is."

"She's in the workshop," I tell Danielsen over the phone, as Aron slips through the gears and accelerates between the warehouses and stacks of shipping containers on the perimeter of the new harbour. The emergency lights flash across the corrugated metal sides of the container, and I reach across the dashboard to turn them off. "Slow down, Aron," I say, as we approach an icy corner in the road. "Stop here."

The tyres crunch in the snow as we stop just above the charred roof of a car workshop. It has been abandoned ever since the fire. Insurance has always been a luxurious concept for many Greenlanders, including the owners of the workshop. It will rot, slowly, like many privately-owned buildings and houses dotted around the coast of Greenland, until an outside investor sees potential in the space and pulls it down.

I scan the surroundings and see a small path beaten through the snow to the back door. It leads all the way to the road. I can see the start of the path in the beam of the patrol car's headlights.

"Ma'am," Danielsen says. "Where are you?"

"I'm looking at the workshop. I left the Jonkheer in one of the cells at the station."

"Wait there. We're coming to you."

I lower the phone as I squint at thin lines of light seeping through the black timber walls of the workshop.

"Someone's inside," I say.

"And we're coming to you."

The back door opens and the light floods out onto the snow, illuminating the figure of a man dressed in a black police uniform.

"Aron," I say. "The lights."

It's too late. Ooqi slams the workshop door and the light is extinguished.

"Commissioner?" Danielsen's voice recedes as I lower the phone and reach for the door handle. "Petra?"

"Aron, give me your gun," I say, as I open the car door.

"Shouldn't we wait, ma'am?"

"Just give it to me."

It might be the adrenaline coursing through my

body, but it feels like he is too slow, and I snatch the Glock pistol from his hand as I step out of the car.

"Stay here and wait for Danielsen," I say, as I tighten the elastic securing my hair in a ponytail.

I can hear Aron's mobile ring as I turn mine off and stuff it into my pocket. The snow is slippery at the top of the path, and I slide into the drift to one side, scramble to my feet, switch the Glock to my right hand, and run down the path. I slow to a walk, arms extended, both hands around the pistol, as I approach the back door of the workshop.

I can smell the burned wood, and something else, like cooking odours through the timbers. I reach for the door handle with one hand and open it, just an inch, and then three more. It's black like a winter sky inside, as I open the door just wide enough to step inside.

My heart is beating so fast it feels like the echoes are bouncing off the black blistered walls, pummelling my body as I move further into the workshop. I bump a desk with my thigh and something rolls off and thuds on the floor. I freeze, press my hands around the pistol grip, and slowly lift my foot to take another step.

I don't know how I turned it on, but *practical me* runs through a quick assessment of what I know about Ooqi, and what he is capable of. Taking Quaa was a rash move, something I forced him to do. All the other victims had already suffered. They were already dead. I once called the Calendar Man an opportunistic coward, but I realise now that I was wrong. There was nothing *opportunistic* about Ooqi's actions and *coward* doesn't seem to fit either. If what the Jonkheer said is true, Ooqi was following orders, using a recipe designed to achieve the greatest effect at a minimal cost.

An effective, rational, deliberate and cool campaign.

I only hope he will remain cool, now that I have pushed him off course. Now that he has Quaa.

The timber floor cracks beneath my boot and I jump at the sound. My sudden movement draws a figure out of the shadow and I feel a whoosh of air a second before something heavy slams into my shoulder and I spin onto the floor. My left hand submerges through a film of litter and ash, as I break my fall. The Glock is heavy in my right hand, and I turn it in an arc, following the sound of someone crashing through the debris on the workshop floor. I squeeze the trigger safety, squeezing further until I fire the first bullet, followed by a second and a third, shattering the silence and splintering the walls of the workshop. I hear a shout, a curse, and the back door as it is kicked open and he is gone.

My boots slip in the debris as I pick myself up. I'm tempted to run after Ooqi, but a cry from above stops me, and I pull out my phone to use it as a torch. There is a metal staircase to my right, the steps creak as I climb it, drifting the light from my phone ahead of me as I carefully place my feet.

When my light catches the sooty face of a young girl, I lower the Glock, stuffing it into my jacket pocket as I pick my way across broken floorboards, avoiding the ragged holes in the floor until I am right in front of Quaa.

"It's okay," I say, as I hold out my hand. "I've got you. You're okay now."

I press the tips of my fingers into the dirty

blanket covering her body, and then I press my hand around her arm and pull her to my body. Quaa flings her arms around my neck and presses her face into my cheek. I can feel snot and tears on my skin as I clasp a hand behind her head and another beneath her bottom, tugging her into my chest as I work my way to the stairs.

"I'm going to take you home, Quaa. Okay?"

I pause at the top of the stairs as lights flicker in solid beams of white through the workshop below. The lights mounted to the SRU's submachine guns pick through the ash and dust until they find us, and I turn my face into the beam, so they can see it is me. I turn around and the light catches Quaa. A second later and the first of the SRU officers is on the stairs and I let him guide us down and through the workshop door and around the front to where Danielsen is waiting. He walks beside us as a paramedic gently plucks Quaa from my arms to examine her, while his partner turns me in the light to look at my cheek.

"I'm alright," I say. "He hit my shoulder."

"We need to look," the man says.

I smile at Quaa as I follow her inside the ambulance. Danielsen waits at the door.

"Aron said he heard shots," he says.

"Yes. I fired three times."

"That explains the blood in the snow." He points at the path leading to the back of the workshop. "You must have hit him."

"Yes."

"And did you see his face? Was it Ooqi?"

"I think so. He was wearing a police uniform. But I didn't actually see him."

Danielsen nods as Atii jogs across the snow from the workshop to the ambulance. She removes her ballistic helmet and mask and lets the submachinegun dangle from the sling around her chest.

"It looks like he's been here a lot," she says. "We need more light, but we found three chest freezers in the back. They're not plugged in, but there are body parts in one of them, and a bloody knife on a workbench. There's also a stack of advent calendars."

"The Commissioner says she shot him," Danielsen says.

"I think it was him," I say.

"Okay." Atii waves one of the SRU officers over. "Start the search from here and put units on all the roads." She looks at the black water and then at the lights of Chinatown glowing on the other side of the fjord. "Get a water unit here too. He might have a boat."

"What about Natuk?" I say.

"No sign of her yet," Danielsen says.

"We need to find her."

"*Aap*. But right now, we need to get you and Quaa home. You need some rest. I'll call you the minute we hear anything."

"The very minute…"

"Yes, ma'am," he says. "Aron will follow you in the patrol car."

I reach out for Quaa as the paramedic closes the door. There is a faint trace of coconut in her hair as I press my lips to her brow.

"You're going to be okay, Quaa. Let's get you home."

Marlunngorneq

Tuesday, 23rd December 2042

Chapter 23

Greenlandic culture is full of powerful creatures, beasts and spirits. The Danish Christmas tradition is heavily influenced by *nisser*, Christmas elves in all nuances of good and evil to the downright mischievous. The Greenlandic Christmas tradition includes a bit of both, but I have never imagined Christmas to be a time of dragons. But when Danielsen calls from the patrol car on the street outside Iiluuna's apartment, I look out of the kitchen window and I can see Tan Yazhu sitting in the passenger seat.

"Iiluuna," I say, as I finish the call. "I have to go."

Quaa is sleeping on Iiluuna's lap on the sofa. She is safe now. One of Gaba's security men is in the hall outside the apartment, and I must leave. If it is possible to save one more person before Christmas, I owe it to Ooqi to at least try.

"Will you come back?"

"As soon as I can."

"*Aap*," she says. "I meant will you come for Christmas Eve?"

Quaa stirs on her mother's lap and opens one of her soft brown eyes.

"Yes," I say. "There's nowhere else I would rather be."

Quaa smiles and I fix her image in my mind as I grab my jacket and leave the apartment. It's only when I stuff my hands into the pocket and feel the twist of twine between my fingers that I realise it is David's. I can't remember how long I have been wearing it, if I had it on when Gaba and I were at the

Ombudsman's house, or if I wore it when I shot Ooqi. Appearances don't matter, I realise. All that matters is that he is with me.

Danielsen meets me on the path to the street. He stops me with a nod towards the patrol car.

"There's been a sighting in Chinatown, and I thought he might come in useful."

"He's not armed?"

"No, and he's willing to drop all charges and pretend it never happened. I think someone has leaned on him from above."

"Lucky for us."

"*Aap.* But we're not done yet. Atii has Chinatown locked down, and Gaba's men are all over Nuuk and Little Amsterdam." Danielsen shakes his head. "I don't know where he gets them from. They're like *nisser.*"

"It's Âmo," I say. "He's looking out for us."

"Whoever and however, the First Minister is happy, and voting has begun."

"And Natuk?"

"Still no sign. If she's involved and if she's smart…"

"She'll be long gone," I say. "What are the chances of both of them joining the force and keeping their family relationship secret?"

"Good, apparently, ma'am."

"Yes," I say, and take a step towards the car. "Let's go and get him."

Atii's security cordon is tight, with a ring of Âmo security around the first perimeter of armed police officers. There is a team of SRU officers standing in front of the perimeter and six long flame-bright dragons weaving through the crowds. There is a second when I wonder if Atii's perimeter is for Ooqi or to prevent the dragons from slipping out of Chinatown. Under different circumstances I might be tempted to think it was the latter. But bullets and ballistic shields won't stop the Chinese dragon – nothing can.

"Ma'am," Atii says, and pulls me to one side.

"Where is he?"

"He was spotted here," she says, raising her voice over the Chinese horns, drums and gongs as she pulls up a map on her tablet. "He's still in uniform, and he bluffed his way into the Chinese medical centre. They treated him for a bullet wound to the left arm. He said he was shot by the Calendar Man, if you believe that."

"Right now," I say, with a second glance at the dragons, "there's very little I don't believe. But there's only one thing I want to know – what is he going to do?"

"Hard to say, ma'am. He knows he's surrounded, and it's unlikely that he's going to get away. It's just a matter of time before we pick him up." Atii curses as a tall man pushes through the police cordon. "I said no, Gaba," she says.

"And I remember disagreeing."

"He does this all the time, ma'am," Atii says. "He still thinks he's head of the SRU, and that he's still my boss."

"We're married," Gaba says, and shrugs. "Of course, I'm the boss."

"Let's save this for later, and let the Commissioner decide."

"Decide what?"

"Gaba thinks that Ooqi will give himself in, if you talk to him."

"It makes sense, Petra. He has been through your files. He used your past to mislead the investigation…"

"Helped by his sister," I say.

"*Aap.* But nonetheless, there is a connection there. And," Gaba says with a smile, "you shot him."

"Gaba thinks he'll talk to you, if you're alone – no visible police presence. Danielsen and I agree, reluctantly."

I look over my shoulder and see Danielsen fastening a bulletproof vest around Tan Yazhu's body. He nods and points at two more vests on the roof of the SUV.

"And you have a plan?"

"Tan Yazhu will take you into Chinatown, through the festival to the location where Ooqi was last seen."

"The medical centre?"

"A noodle bar, just in front of it," she says. "Gaba has forced me to agree that he should go with you."

"For old time's sake," he says, and grins. "And, I'm bored."

"I left you in charge of the kids," Atii says.

"They're teenagers. They don't need me anymore, babe."

I let them quarrel as I walk back to Danielsen. He hands me a vest and I remove David's jacket and pull the vest over my head.

"I recognise this jacket," Danielsen says, as he helps me with the vest.

"You've seen me wear it before."

"*Aap*. But I never thought about it. It's Maratse's, isn't it?"

I nod. "It makes me feel safe."

I zip David's jacket over my vest and wait as Danielsen explains to Tan Yazhu the very limit of his involvement.

"Aqqa," I say, when he is finished. "I need to know – you've done everything you can to keep me out of harm's way, right up until this moment. But now, you're just going to let me walk in there? Why?"

"Because no matter what he's done, ma'am, and for whatever reason, Ooqi is one of ours, and I think you can bring him home." Danielsen removes his pistol from the holster at his belt and presses it into my hand. "Besides, I know you can take care of yourself," he says. Danielsen looks at Gaba. "And he'll never let anything happen to you."

"That's a lot of responsibility, Aqqa."

"It goes with the title," he says.

"You don't want to be Commissioner?"

"Never have, never will." He pats his belly and laughs. "Besides, my wife would never let me. The hours you keep…"

I stuff Aqqa's pistol inside my jacket pocket and dip my head, just once.

"I'll be here when you get back," he says.

Tan Yazhu walks beside me to the edge of the police perimeter. His eyes are fixed on the dragons, and the end of the street where a little slice of his home country is nestled between the granite rocks of Greenland. Gaba presses the Velcro straps of his vest into position and lifts the flap of a canvas holster attached at an angle to the front of the vest.

"What's that?" I ask, as he winks at Atii and we

move through the cordon and into a corridor of flame and dragons.

"A shotgun," he says.

"You're armed."

"It's legal. It's for hunting."

"You've sawn off the stock and shortened the barrel, Gaba."

He shrugs. "It didn't fit in the pouch."

"This way," Tan Yazhu says, as he weaves around the dragons swirling in the street.

I can feel the beat of the drums through the asphalt, and the echo between the tall buildings, brushing at the snow on the roofs. The beat makes it difficult to think, and I worry that I'm not prepared, that I can't help Ooqi after all, and that he is beyond reach. But there is no more time to think, as Tan Yazhu raises his hand and points through the crowds towards the noodle bar at the edge of the street. The bright plastic tables shine in the light of Chinese lanterns, and the snow is coloured in reds and yellows, the colours of flame and fire. Between the flames I see Ooqi. I see the bandage around his arm, the sling around his neck, and the empty sleeve of his jacket dangling at his side.

"Danielsen say I must stop here," Tan Yazhu says. "But I will come if you want me to."

"No," I say. "You've done enough."

"You will stop him," he says. "I trust you now."

Gaba waits until he is gone and then points to a position close to Ooqi's table.

"I'll stay close," he says.

"I know."

I can't hear my words for the beating of the drums. Or is it the thumping of my heart? It beats faster as Ooqi turns his head and catches my eye. I'm close enough to see his eyes flicker behind the lenses of his glasses, and I wonder if he is online, if he is connected with Natuk, and if this is all a trap. He could be streaming it. This could be his last chance to strike before voting is over, but there is something else in his eyes. Sadness.

Piitalaat. Focus.

I wondered when David would come. I know it is me, that I am projecting what I want to hear, but it gives me the courage to take the next step, and the one after that until I am standing at Ooqi's table, and he invites me to sit down.

"Just a second," he says, as his eyes flicker. He removes his glasses and puts them on the table. "That was Natuk. She's gone. You have to promise you won't try to find her."

"Is she involved?"

"No. It was all me."

He's lying, of course he is. The twitch beneath his eye that shudders through his soft, young cheek betrays more than the lie. I can see his love for his sister, and he's willing to make that last sacrifice. I realise I might never know about her role in the Calendar Man's campaign of terror. At least, not from Ooqi.

"I need to know why," I say.

"Why?"

"Why did you try to stop the vote?"

"You have to ask?" He gestures at the festival behind us, raises his voice over the beat of the drums. "Do you think we can negotiate all this? You think we can decide our own future?"

"I think we have the right to try."

"You're wrong," he says. "Think about it. Greenland never had an industrial revolution. We haven't had a gradual progression from one technology to the next. We went from turf huts to apartment blocks, from hunting with harpoons to checking the weather on our smartphones. Greenland went global too fast too soon." He shakes his head. "We can't process this. We don't have the experience. We can't do it alone. We need help."

"Then we ask for help."

"And whose help will we get? Who will help us to understand the nuances of a seventy-page contract in a foreign language?"

"You sound like your foster mother. That's what she would say."

Perhaps he doesn't know that we have her in custody, or perhaps he doesn't know that the Jonkheer is ready to make a statement detailing how the Ombudsman Anna Riis had a plan to spoil the vote and ensure that Greenland remained a part of Denmark for the foreseeable future. But he's still ready to fall on his sword for her. I can see it in his eyes.

"She's got nothing to do with this," he says.

"Ooqi," I say. "I understand that she helped you. She helped both of you. And I realise how loyal that makes you feel, that you owe her. But you don't, Ooqi. You don't have to take responsibility for this, just to protect her."

"No-one was hurt," he says.

"You terrorised the people of Nuuk and frightened the whole country."

"No-one died. There were no victims, I made sure of that."

"Victims? What about their families, their friends? What about Quaa?"

"No," he says, as he pushes back from the table. "That was your fault. I was done. The referendum was finished. But you, you had to ruin *everything*."

Ooqi's last word turns the heads of the people eating at the next table. It snaps Gaba to attention and he reaches for the flap covering the shotgun on his vest. There is a flash of dragons reflected in the window of the noodle bar behind Ooqi, and I'm distracted by the beat of the drum. I don't see Ooqi pull the pistol from his holster, not until it is inches from my face. The diners at the nearby tables spill their noodles as they flee into the street. There is a scream, almost swallowed by the drum and the dragon, but then the crowd withdraws, the beat slows to an echo, and it's just Ooqi, Gaba and me.

"Ooqi," I say. "Please."

"I thought you would understand," he says. "I read your file. I've seen your hands. You've suffered. More than me, maybe more than Natuk. I thought you would know that we need someone strong to take care of us. We can't do this alone. We shouldn't be alone."

"Being independent doesn't mean we have to be alone, Ooqi. Whatever she told you, whatever she taught you, you're not alone."

"You leave her out of this." Spittle flies from Ooqi's mouth as he stands and jabs the gun closer to my face. "She saved us. And this," he says, waving the gun at the terrified people on the street. "It was the least I could do."

I glance at Gaba. He has the shotgun out of the holster and his fingers curled around the grip. Ooqi twists his head to see where I am looking, and then lurches backwards. I grab for his jacket, tug at the loose sleeve. Ooqi spins and twists out of his jacket. His pistol thumps into the snow at his feet as he pulls his arm free. He reaches for it.

"Leave it," Gaba yells, as he moves to within just a few feet of Ooqi.

I pull the pistol from my pocket and walk around the side of the table.

"Ooqi," I say. "This is my friend, Gaba. He used to be a policeman. He's one of us. He won't hurt you. I won't let him. Just move back, away from the gun."

I relax my grip and lower Danielsen's pistol, just a little, as Ooqi looks into my eyes, and then past me, towards the table. I turn my head a fraction and see the reflection of the Chinese lanterns in Ooqi's glasses. He nods once, and then reaches for the gun.

"No," I shout, as he curls his hand around the pistol grip and raises the barrel towards me.

No drum is louder than the simultaneous blast of the two shells in Gaba's shotgun, and a bullet from the pistol in my own hands. But I wish the drums would beat, and the dragons roar, because the silence is killing me just as I killed Ooqi.

In that minute I don't care about the vote, and I don't care about Greenland, because all I can think about is that I only had one thing to do, and I failed. I failed to bring him home.

Pingasunngorneq

Wednesday, 24th December 2042

Christmas Eve

Chapter 24

If I open my eyes, I can see the red glow of the paper star in Quaa's window. *If* I open my eyes. I don't want to, but I have slept too long already. I can hear Iiluuna preparing a late breakfast in the kitchen, and Quaa's voice – higher than her mother's – asking if *now* was a good time to wake Petra. I suppose now is as good a time as any, and I open my eyes.

It's better than I thought. Quaa's room is familiar – the posters on the wall, the toys she says she is too old for, the clothes she should have tidied away, the smell of the duvet – soft and warm. Everything is reassuringly familiar, and very far from the blood red snow outside the noodle bar in Chinatown.

I checked with the duty officer shortly before I crawled into Quaa's bed. Even after the death of her foster son, Anna Riis remains silent, and I suppose she will stay that way until her lawyers arrive sometime after Christmas. The Jonkheer's statement provided just enough evidence to keep her in her cell until they turn up. The duty officer promised to keep me updated through the day.

It's time to get up.

I have some clothes in the bottom drawer in Quaa's room, and I dress in the soft glow of the star. The Northern Lights are bright, drifting and twisting above Nuuk in greens and pale blues. If we're lucky we might get a little red light, just for Christmas. Beyond the city I can just see the black fjord, the icebergs in the bay, and a single fishing trawler returning to the harbour with the last catch before Christmas.

Quaa skips across the kitchen floor in bare feet as

I open the door and step out of her room. She wraps her arms around my waist, and I smooth her hair – she is coconut clean for Christmas. And she is wearing her crown of pine and candles. She is transformed from the girl Ooqi held captive in the ashes and black timbers of the workshop. Quaa tips her head back and starts talking. I don't hear the words. Instead I search for some sign of trauma, but she is giddy with Christmas and I have to see the tree.

She tugs me into the living room, her small hand clasping my fingers, and she presents the tree, only slightly taller than she is.

"It's very pretty," I say, as she turns on the lights – small white buds between the baubles and the paper streamers of Greenlandic flags.

There is a star on top.

It makes me think of Ooqi, and David, and I bend down to hug Quaa, so she can't see my tears.

There's more to see, and I let her lead me around the apartment, pointing out various ornaments and the all-important *nisser*, tiny felt or plastic Christmas elves peeking out from behind picture frames, tucked behind the furniture, and posed between the candles on the kitchen table. We stop here. Quaa pulls out a chair, presses me into it, and pushes another so close I have to move my fingers before they are pinched. Quaa has something in her hands, beneath the table, and I pretend I cannot see it.

"Christmas tea," Iiluuna says, as she joins us. She places a pot on the table and slides a mug across the heart-themed table cloth. The air is spiced with cinnamon, orange and steam as she pours.

"Thank you."

"She can't wait," she says, as Quaa slips the

present from her lap to the table.

"Is this for me?"

"*Aap.*"

The small box is heavy in my hands. Quaa's eyes are bright like stars as she watches my face. The bows are loose, and the wrapping is torn in places, but the paper filling inside the cardboard box is generous and I tease Quaa with an astonished smile.

"Paper. Oh, Quaa, it's just what I wanted."

Her hands jerk from her lap. She can't help herself, and then the top layer of paper is loose on the table and I see a small dark soapstone figure inside. It's a hunter sitting on his sledge. Quaa helps me take him out of the box. There are two dogs, and they clink together at the end of thick cotton threads as if they are pulling the hunter across the ice.

"It's David," she says. "We bought it at the Christmas market."

I don't even try to hide the tears, as I push back my chair to make room for Quaa to crawl into my lap.

"Thank you," I whisper into her hair.

Iiluuna reaches around the candles on the table and places an ornamental flag pole made of wood beside the hunter on his sledge. Her eyes sparkle and widen, tugging the corners of her mouth into a smile. I can feel my brow tighten as I frown at the flag.

"*Erfalasorput,*" she says. "Our flag."

I've forgotten something. Quaa wriggles in my lap and slides across to her chair as I stare at the red and white flag, the symbol of the red sun rising over the white ice. And then it comes to me, and I see the hunter, picture him sledging across the ice towards the sun, and I realise that the people of Greenland have voted.

Iiluuna turns on the radio and I hear a mix of Greenlandic and Danish chatter, comments spliced between and around the First Minister's speech. Iiluuna turns up the volume.

"My favourite bit," she says, and we listen.

… *Greenland for all Greenlanders, for our children, their children and all our futures.*

We both look at Quaa as she plays with the hunter on his sledge, moving the dogs across the heart-patterned ice, one in both hands, her long black hair framing her cheeks, and the flag of Greenland, *Erfalasorput*, reflected in her eyes.

Later, we will sing Christmas carols and hymns as we hold hands and dance around the tree – a Danish tradition, loved and unlikely to be forgotten, like so many Greenlandic things rooted in a colonial history. We will remember the good things, and the bad, and look to the future. But I need some fresh air before then, and I need to buy gifts for Iiluuna and Quaa, and I need a quiet time, just for David and me.

It is quiet at the graveyard. I stuff my hands inside the deep pockets of David's jacket and fiddle with the twine between my fingers. The sky is grey with snow, and I can feel the first flakes as they fall softly onto my hair. Everything is still and quiet, and I don't hear the footsteps behind me, only the cough as Qitu clears his throat not to startle me.

"I haven't seen you for a while," I say, as he smiles.

"You've kept me busy though."

"*I* have?"

"*Aap*," he says, and then points to the small metal

Greenlandic flag pinned to his collar. "There was a tiny bit of other news. I have a meeting with the First Minister later."

"It's a big day."

"It doesn't get much bigger."

Qitu reaches into his pocket and takes out a gift. The wrapping, and the bow, is only slightly neater than Quaa's.

"For you," he says.

"I didn't get you anything, Qitu."

"You don't have to."

He watches my face as I unwrap a small photo frame, hinged in the middle. I stuff the paper into my pocket and slowly open the frame. The boy in the picture on the right is Ooqi. I recognise his nose, and his eyes. He's wearing the furs of a hunter and holding a huge fish between his hands. It's too heavy for him and he grins at the weight of it. Natuk is in the picture on the left, also in furs – perhaps from the same day. I can just see Ooqi behind her. She is laughing at something.

"Atti asked me to see what I could find," Qitu says. "This is from Upernavik. Their family is from there. They must have visited one time. A happier time," he says. "I thought you might want to remember him like that."

"You're going to write a longer piece about him, aren't you?"

"*Aap.*"

"You have to use this photo," I say. "Both of them."

"I will."

"Thank you."

Qitu slips quietly through the snow after I hug

him, and I slip the photo frame inside David's cavernous pockets. It really is amazing how deep they are, and I have a sudden image of Âmo, pressing his abnormally long arms into deep pockets, all the way to his toes. The thought makes me laugh.

It's good to hear you laugh, Piitalaat.

"It feels good," I say.

You're going to be alright.

"I think I might be, someday."

I know you will.

I can feel a tear on my cheek and I wipe it away with my finger.

"I have to leave you now. You know that."

Iiji.

"I'll come back, when I can."

I know.

I wipe away a second tear and crouch in the snow beside David's gravestone. The plastic flowers are bright against the snow and I brush a dusting of fresh snowflakes from the leaves. David is quiet as I sit there, my bottom on my heels, my knees pressed into the snow, and my hands stuffed into David's pockets. That's when I see it, the black cylinder resting on the granite shelf at the bottom of the gravestone.

The cylinder is metal. If we were further north, if it was colder, it might stick to my fingers. But the cylinder has a coat of paint, and the cap unscrews without protest, without the cold bite and stiffness I expect. Perhaps it was left here recently. Perhaps someone left it here today.

"Did you see them, David?" I ask. But he is silent. *I* am silent, and sad that I am ready to move on.

Not so the person who left the note rolled tight

inside the cylinder.

And what should I do in Illyria? My brother he is in Elysium.

The text is printed on one line, lengthways, small. It is almost lost in the middle of the sheet of paper.

She was here. Natuk. She left this, I'm sure of it.

I roll the paper between my fingers and seal it inside the cylinder. It might be evidence one day, and I sigh at the thought of my fingerprints smearing the cylinder, contaminating it. But then my fingerprints are all over this case, and any future case that might be linked to it.

"I can't worry about that now," I say, as I stand up and brush the snow from my knees. It is falling heavier now, as the day grows darker. I should get back. I should help Iiluuna with the Christmas dinner.

I put the cylinder in my pocket, lift the flowers above the snow, and press my fingers on the cold granite headstone.

"I'll be back, David. Often," I say.

A pillow of wind fluffs at the snow as I leave the graveyard and wait in line for one of Nuuk's yellow buses. The passengers chatter and smile, and it is more than just the magic of Christmas. There is a streak of independence in the air, tempered with the unknown, yet light, buoyed by optimism and dreams.

I can hear the First Minister's words on the radio, but my thoughts settle on Quaa's gift, the hunter on the kitchen table, the hunter on the ice, the sun rising in the north, shining red on its return. Christmas in Greenland marks the turning of the year, when the nights grow shorter. It is still pitch black in the far north, but even there, people can see a shade of grey growing lighter at end of each night.

After so many dark days, the light is returning, for the hunter and his dogs, for me, and for people of Greenland – independent and free.

The End

About the Author

Christoffer Petersen is the author's pen name. He lives in Denmark. Chris started writing stories about Greenland while teaching in Qaanaaq, the largest village in the very north of Greenland – the population peaked at 600 during the two years he lived there. Chris spent a total of seven years in Greenland, teaching in remote communities and at the Police Academy in the capital of Nuuk.

Chris continues to be inspired by the vast icy wilderness of the Arctic and his books have a common setting in the region, with a Scandinavian influence. He has also watched enough Bourne movies to no longer be surprised by the plot, but not enough to get bored.

You can find Chris in Denmark or online here:

www.christoffer-petersen.com

CHRISTOFFER PETERSEN

By the same author:

THE GREENLAND CRIME SERIES
featuring Constable David Maratse

Book 1
SEVEN GRAVES, ONE WINTER

Book 2
BLOOD FLOE

Book 3
WE SHALL BE MONSTERS

Short stories from the same series
KATABATIC
CONTAINER
TUPILAQ
THE LAST FLIGHT
THE HEART THAT WAS A WILD GARDEN

and

THE GREENLAND TRILOGY
featuring Konstabel Fenna Brongaard

Book 1
THE ICE STAR

Book 2
IN THE SHADOW OF THE MOUNTAIN

Book 3
THE SHAMAN'S HOUSE